CYNTHIA HICKEY

THE TEACHER'S RESCUE
Book 2 in Finding Love in Disaster

Cynthia Hickey

Copyright 2015
Written by: Cynthia Hickey
Published by: Winged Publications
Cover Design: Cynthia Hickey

This book is a work of fiction. Names, characters, places, and incidents are the product of the author's imagination and are used fictitiously. Any resemblance to actual events, locales, or persons, living or dead, is coincidental.

No part of this book may be copied or distributed without the author's consent.
All rights reserved.

ISBN-13: 979-8-8690-8660-0

DEDICATION

To all the wonderful readers who so enjoyed the first book in my Finding Love in Disaster. Thank you!.

THE TEACHER'S RESCUE

1

"Are you sure you'll be all right staying home alone?" Emma Larson, the new school teacher in the small town of Oakton, Missouri, bent and peered into her grandmother's face. Having recently moved in with her grandmother in order to help the poor dear who had a tendency to get lost in a town of only one thousand people, Emma feared leaving her while she headed to work.

"I managed just fine before you got here." Grandma pulled the knitted shawl tighter around her shoulders. "I think I can manage not to die in the next few hours."

Emma wasn't so sure, but grabbed her new leather purse, pinned a jaunty blue hat on her head, and sailed out the door anyway. Her new navy crepe silk dress with streamer tie left her feeling confident enough to face the one room schoolhouse and twenty students.

With a bounce to her step, she headed down the road and toward the end of town where the white washed building shone like a diamond in the sky. She'd have her work cut out for her since the school had lacked a teacher for over a month, but she could do this with God's help. That and her sheer will not to fail.

She passed a storefront where a man swept the walk under a shingle that said, "Doctor Baxter." He glanced up at her with eyes as blue as the sun and hair the color of ripened wheat. She returned his smile, her cheeks heating. It had been a long time since a handsome man looked at her like that. Not since her former fiancé, anyway. That was another reason she'd chosen to come live with Grandma. Why stay in St. Louis, where heartache lived?

"You must be the new schoolteacher," the man said, setting aside his broom. "I'm Doc Baxter."

"How can you tell by looking at me that I'm the schoolteacher?" Emma cocked her head.

"I can tell a lot by looking at you." A dimple winked in his cheek.

Well, Emma could flirt with the best of them. She tilted her head back to get a better look at him. "Such as?"

He chuckled. "You're excited about your first day, much like most of your students I've talked to. You're courageous for one so young." He stared harder.

Her pulse raced.

"And, I'd give my best hat if you didn't have a heart as big as the Ozarks."

"You're only saying that because I've come to take care of my grandmother." She clutched her purse tighter. "Thank you for the compliment, but I don't want to be late on my first day. I'm Emma Larson, by the way." She strolled down the walk, the grin never fading from her face.

The sun dappled the sidewalk through branches emerging with spring green. Birds serenaded from a large oak tree in the schoolyard. While the air still carried a tiny bite from winter, the first day of teaching in a new school could not be more beautiful.

Emma dug the key out of her purse, climbed seven steps, and unlocked the door. Inside, twenty desks sat in neat rows. A wood burning stove occupied the back corner next to a large chalkboard behind the teacher's desk. Another door, open to reveal hooks and shelves for students to hang coats and store lunch pails, was on the other side. An American flag stood proudly beside the door. Windows lined both outside walls. Emma couldn't ask for anything better. It was perfect.

She walked across the floor. Boards in the center of the room echoed her footsteps. She glanced down. A trap door had been set in the middle of the room. They were in the Ozarks, after all. Most likely the town founders thought it necessary to install a storm cellar. She shrugged. Most people built the entrances to cellars on the outside of buildings, but it reassured her to know the school had one.

After storing her purse in a drawer of her desk, she grabbed a piece of chalk and wrote Miss Larson in big scrawling letters. Under that, she listed the day's spelling words and math problems, putting each grade in a separate column. When she finished, she had ten minutes to spare and stepped outside in preparation of ringing the bell. At five minutes before the beginning of school, she rang it to give the five minute warning.

Students, ranging in age from six to fifteen, dashed into the yard. Emma's heart swelled. For eight hours a day, they were hers to teach, nurture, and protect. There was no greater responsibility outside of being a mother. She glanced heavenward and gave a prayer of thanks before ringing the final bell to start the day.

The students sat according to grade level, starting with the youngest in front. Emma moved to the front of the room and stood, hands folded in front of her, until the room quieted. "Good morning. I am Miss Larson, your teacher. Each morning, your spelling words and math problems will be written on the board. First thing, once you're seated, is to copy these in your notebooks. Then, we will proceed with reading."

A little blond girl in the front row raised her hand. "I can't read."

Emma smiled. "I will help the younger students. Now, let's proceed with roll call so I can acquaint myself with you."

She picked up the roll sheet from her desk and read the names out loud, committing each face and name to memory. A young red-haired boy in the front row, Tommy Baxter, grinned impishly up at her. She wondered whether he might be the doctor's son, and felt shame that she might have flirted with a married man. She shook off the humiliating thought, took a deep breath, and continued.

"Tommy Baxter!" The little imp plunged his neighbor's pigtail into his inkwell. "Come up here and face the chalkboard. You'll remain after school for your behavior, and I'll be speaking with your father."

Tommy stuck his tongue out at the other students and ran to the board. Emma handed him a piece of chalk. "Start writing, I will not bother the other students, fifty times." She wrote the sentence at the top for him to copy.

He sighed. "I don't care. I can write a hundred if you want."

She had no idea how to respond to such a

comment. Hopefully, his parents could give her guidance. Handing out discipline was not strange to her, she'd been teaching for five years, but to have a student, even one so young, openly defy her, was not something she had dealt with before.

"You will also stay in for recess." She turned to the rest of the class. "As spring quickly approaches, I thought it might be fun for us to put on a spring recital. As we disperse for lunch and recess, I hope you will be thinking of ideas. We will continue in thirty minutes."

The class stampeded for their lunch pails and headed outside, leaving Emma with a sullen six-year-old boy. "Sit at your desk and eat, Tommy." Emma took her own seat and unwrapped a simple cheese sandwich.

Tommy fetched his pail and set out a thermos, an apple, and a sandwich with cheese and meat. Obviously, his doctor father could provide well in the food department. Hopefully, Tommy's lack of discipline was not the absence of parental concern, but rather the testing of a new teacher.

Lunchtime inside passed in silence, the only sound, the laughter of children playing outside. Tommy glanced at the window a couple of times, but resumed his eating without comment. What type of child did not beg to go outside and play?

Sadness clouded his features, wrenching at Emma's heart. "Tommy, is there something you want to tell me? Is there a reason for your misbehavior?"

Without glancing up, he said, "My mama is dead."

~

Jesse stood outside his office and watched the town's children parade past, lunch pails swinging, but no Tommy. He groaned. Either his son had wandered off daydreaming or had been held after school. He was going with the latter. He flipped a sign on the window to back in a few minutes, then locked the door before marching down the street and to the school house.

Sure enough, his son wiped down the chalkboard, using a stool in order to reach the top. Somehow, he doubted Tommy did so out of the kindness of his heart.

Miss Larson glanced up from her desk. "Mr. Baxter, thank you for coming. This is better than me bringing Tommy home. Please, have a seat."

Jesse squeezed his six-foot four bulk into one of the desks. "What's he done?"

She frowned. "You don't seem surprised."

"I'm not. My son is a rascal."

She opened her mouth to say something, then closed it and took a deep breath. She glanced at her hands, then back up at him. "He told me his mother died. I'm sorry. Was it recent?"

"Almost two years ago." While the pain of her passing had lessened, Jesse's heart still lurched when someone mentioned his loss. "Tommy hasn't been the same since."

His son turned and glared at him. Jesse shrugged. He would deal with the behavior when they returned home. He again asked what his son did to warrant being held after school.

"It started with him dipping Sarah's pigtails in ink. Then, he back-talked me when I ordered him to write sentences. He has been punished, Mr. Baxter. I don't feel further discipline is needed, but I did want you to be aware of the behavior and to let me know that you support my discipline procedures."

"I support you wholeheartedly." Jesse could use all the help he could get. "My office hours leave Tommy bored and restless a lot of the time. I'm hoping that regular schooling will help curb some of his energy."

"That is a temporary fix, Mr. Baxter." She frowned. "There are only a few more months of school left. What will you do in the summer? Allow him to run free at will?"

Jesse scratched his head. "I'll have to hire someone to watch him. Are you insinuating that my son doesn't take priority in my life?"

"Not at all. I'm not familiar enough with either of you to make such assumptions." She stood and halted Tommy's wiping of the board. "You may go home now." She bent to put herself at his eye level. "Tomorrow is a new day. I hope it is a better one."

Jesse admired her ability to forgive, but he still intended to merit discipline of his own once he got his son home. "Let's go. Thank you for your time, Miss Larson."

"Thank you for coming, Mr. Baxter." She walked them to the door.

"I'm very disappointed in you, son." Jesse took Tommy's hand. "Because of your disobedience, I have chores for you at the office. What's the matter? Don't you like Miss Larson?"

"She's nice enough."

"Then what is it?"

"She ain't ma." Tommy's chin quivered. "She don't have the right to tell me what to do."

Jesse stopped and knelt, forcing his son to look at him. "You're right. She *isn't* your mother, she's your teacher. That gives her the right to tell you what to do."

He pulled Tommy close, tucking his head under his chin. He closed his eyes and exhaled deeply, wanting to take away his son's pain, but had no idea how.

"Don't you think your ma would want you to be good at school?"

"Yes, sir." Tommy sniffed.

"Then, you owe it to her to be the best you can be." He held him at arm's length. "Can you do that?"

Tommy nodded. "I'll try. But Sarah told me I was a dummy because I spelled my name wrong."

"Did you tell Miss Larson that?"

"No."

"Well, you should have, but it still doesn't make your own actions okay." He resumed leading his hurting child home. "Tell me something good that happened at school today."

"We're going to have a spring recital. I need to find something to do."

"Any ideas what?"

"I'm going to write a poem to ma." Tommy grinned up at him. "Won't she like that?"

Jesse blinked back tears. "She would have loved it." He might not be the best father in the world, but he must be doing something right. He swung Tommy onto his shoulders and continued their walk to his office.

A woman and small child sat on the bench out front, the child holding a large bowl on his lap. "Run next door and do your homework, son. The garbage can wait. Mrs. Morrison, what can I do for you?"

"Leroy won't stop throwing up, Doc. I don't know what else to do."

Jesse opened the door. "Come in. Let's see if we can figure out the problem." He motioned for the boy to sit on the examining table in the back room. "Have you eaten anything today that didn't sit right with you?" He took the child's temperature, only to find it normal.

"My brother and I wanted to see who could eat the most raw eggs. I won." He retched.

"Looks to me like you lost, son." Jesse straightened and pulled a dark-colored bottle from his cabinet. "Give him a teaspoon of this every four hours until he feels better."

"I don't have much money," Mrs. Morrison said. "Will you take a chicken in trade?"

"Pay me when you can. I can set up an installment plan. Don't worry." Jesse led them back to the front room where he wrote down the amount of the doctor's visit.

"I can give you a quarter now, and a quarter a week. Will that be enough?"

Jesse smiled. "That's plenty." He ruffled the boy's hair. "No more raw eggs. You could get more than an upset stomach."

"Yes, sir."

They left, leaving Jesse the rest of the late afternoon to fill out patient reports. At five o'clock, he locked the door, and headed to the house he lived in with Tommy.

"Son?"

"In here." Tommy lay sprawled across his bed, drawing on a pad of paper.

Jesse looked over his son's shoulder to see a picture of a woman lying on top of a patch of grass, flowers clutched in her hands. While the drawing was the rough work of a young child, it wasn't hard to decipher that the picture was of Tommy's mother.

"Son, you've got to let her go. Mommy is in heaven now. She isn't sick anymore."

"I want her here." Tommy tacked the picture to the wall with others of the same. "God doesn't need her. I do."

Jesse sat on the edge of the bed. "You still want her here, knowing how sick she was? How much pain she was in?"

"Yes. I could make her better. You could make her better."

"I couldn't. I tried." The cancer had beaten every doctor's attempts at ridding Maureen of it. "Your mother wouldn't want you focusing on things this way. No more drawing pictures of her dead. You want to draw your mother, then draw her alive and smiling in heaven." Jesse marched from the room.

He was failing as a single father. Perhaps, keeping it just the two of them since his wife's death had been the wrong decision. Maybe it was time for Jesse to look for a wife.

He banged pots in the small kitchen and reached for a crock of soup left by a patient the day before. At the very least, he needed a housekeeper. Someone to cook and clean for them and to mend Tommy's clothing. Jesse had thought he could do it all. How foolish he was. His son needed a woman in his life, even if that woman was only a caretaker.

Lighting the flame on the stove, he straightened, dumped the soup into a pan, and then stared out the window to see Miss Larson making her way home, the setting sun casting highlights on her auburn hair. She was a very lovely woman to lay eyes on, with eyes as dark as coffee and skin that showed she didn't spend a lot of time in the sun.

Maureen had been a fiery redhead, like Tommy, but the new teacher seemed to have an inner fire that simmered like the soup on the stove. He guessed she could explode if pushed far enough, but she had handled Tommy's behavior like a champ.

What would it be like to court a woman like her?

2

The next morning, Emma passed the doctor's office on her way to the school. It didn't escape her attention that she would have to pass that way each morning, or that the handsome doctor could very well be unlocking his door at the exact time she passed. As he was that morning.

"Good morning, Miss Larson."

His dimpled smile did things to her heart that her former fiancée never had.

"Good morning, Mr. Baxter. Tommy." Emma grinned at her student who kicked a rock down the sidewalk. "I find myself in need of an escort this morning. Tommy, may I avail myself of your services?"

He stopped kicking and stared at her as if she'd turned green. "Why are you talking so fancy?"

"Trying to improve your vocabulary. So, will you walk to school with me?"

Tommy shrugged. "I guess." He grabbed his lunch pail off the bench outside the office. "Bye, Dad."

"Have a good day, son." Doctor Baxter ruffled his son's hair, causing him to look like a red-haired porcupine. "Remember ... behave." He bent and whispered something in the boy's ear, then straightened. "Thank you, Miss Larson. I'm usually afraid that he'll be late each morning. He does like to dawdle. Are you sure I can't drive you?"

"The walk will do us good. Come along, Tommy."

He shuffled along behind her, despite her attempts to draw him into a conversation. She skirted the remains of a dead possum, wrinkling her nose at the smell of decay. When she no longer heard Tommy behind her, she turned.

"What do you think killed it?" Tommy asked without looking up. He bent over and peered at the lump of hair and intestines.

"Uh, an automobile?" Oh, dear Lord, now he was poking at the carcass with a stick. "Come, Tommy."

"What if it died of an illness? Can we catch it? Will we die now because we breathed the air?" He gave her a wide-eyed look.

"No, we won't. Come." She gave him her sternest look and forced her stomach not to rebel.

He sighed and followed, dragging the stick in the dirt alongside the road. "My dad wouldn't let me see my mom after she died. Do you think she looked like that?"

Goodness. "I'm sure she didn't. I'm sure she looked as if she were sleeping." The poor dear. He needed the closure seeing his mother would have brought.

"Yeah, I guess. She was sleeping when I went to bed that night, but gone by morning. Dad said she went to sleep and never woke up. Sometimes, I think that will happen to me. Will it?"

Emma stopped and faced him. "Have you discussed your questions about death with your father?"

He shook his head. "He's too busy."

They would see about that. Emma would approach the good doctor immediately after school. Tommy needed his questions answered, and soon. Perhaps she could recommend a book or two from the library suitable for a child of six.

She tried to remember how she had felt when her father died. She had been around Tommy's age. The best she could recall was an overwhelming sense of sadness. If not for her mother and grandma, she would have been lost. Now, all she had was grandma, and while she missed her mother, she was an adult able to deal with her emotions. Tommy was only a child and needed his father's constant reassurance that things would be fine.

"I lost my mother, too," she said. "Would you like to hold my hand?"

He nodded and slipped his already grimy hand into hers. She refused to think of what he might have touched, prayed it hadn't been anything dead, and focused on the sight of the school building ahead of them.

"Would you like to write the first grade spelling words on the board while we wait for the other students?"

"Yes, ma'am!" He released her hand and raced up the stairs to the schoolhouse. She no sooner unlocked the door, than he tossed his lunch pail and jacket at the shelf and thundered toward the chalkboard.

"Tommy, please put your belongings where they belong." Emma peeled off her gloves and hung her coat and satchel on a peg. She quickly jotted the spelling words on a slate and set Tommy to work while she wrote down the words for the other grades.

As the day progressed, Tommy again dipped Sally Biggs pigtails into her ink, stashed a toad in another child's lunch pail, and put dirt in yet another boy's sandwich. By recess, Emma was at her wit's end. While she knew she needed to keep the wayward child inside, she didn't have the strength. Instead, she folded her arms on her desk and rested her head on them.

"Are you ill?"

She raised her head to see Tommy's worried gaze peering down at her. "No, just tired."

"Of my shenanigans?" A frown appeared between his eyes.

"That is definitely part of my exhaustion."

"Why didn't you keep me in from recess?"

"Did you want me to?" Oh. She could almost hear her heart shattering. The poor dear craved her attention and felt the only way he could get it was to misbehave. "What if you go ring the bell letting the others know that recess is over?"

"Yes, ma'am!"

He raced away, leaving Emma more determined than ever to find ways of spending time with the boy. Positive attention was what he needed. That, and the occasional hug for no reason whatsoever.

She had expected him to walk home with her after school, but was delighted to see him run down the road with his classmates, leaving her to clean and lock up. She suspected the child had little time to play, being in trouble so often. In the morning, she would pick him up on her way again and find small chores for him to do in preparation for the start of another school day. The weekends would be more difficult, but if she thought long and hard enough, she could find something for the boy to do around her home.

"Grandma?" Emma hung her coat and purse on the rack beside the front door. "I'm home." She headed to the kitchen, fully expecting to see her grandmother at the stove.

Instead, the kitchen smelled of scorched pan. She turned off the stove and set the ruined saucepan in the sink. "Grandma?"

The screen door banged against the house. Emma's heart lodged in her throat. She'd only heard stories from the neighbors about her grandmother wandering off. That was one of the reasons she had moved to Oakton. Had the poor thing become confused and gone to town?

She glanced to where her grandmother's purse hung. She would never have left her pocketbook behind. Not if she was in her right mind.

Emma jumped from the back stoop, the heel of her shoe sinking into the soft lawn. She tugged free and rushed toward the town's shops. She checked the post office, the dime store, the women's clothing boutique. No one had seen her grandmother in over an hour.

Tears streamed down Emma's face. Where could she look next?

~

"Dr. Baxter!" Miss Larson burst into Jesse's office. Tears streaked her face.

He glanced around to make sure Tommy was still having his afternoon cookies upstairs, then hurried to greet the distraught woman. His gaze quickly scanned over her for signs of injury. Not finding anything visibly wrong, he led her to a chair and lowered her into it.

"What's wrong, Miss Larson? Are you injured?"

She shook her head hard enough to send her hat flying to the floor. "I can't find my grandmother." She grabbed the lapels of his collar. "She gets confused. The neighbors said she sometimes wanders off, but she hasn't since I've come to stay. Please help me find her."

"I'll help you. Tommy!" He called up the stairs. "I need to help Miss Larson with something. You stay here, understand?"

"Yes, sir." Feet pounded overhead.

"You can't leave him home alone." She wiped her eyes with a lace-trimmed hankie she pulled out of her sleeve. "He's barely more than a baby."

"I have a hired woman who comes a few days a week." He helped her to her feet. "She'll stay until I return." He started to take offense at her obvious criticism of his parenting skills, but realized most teachers probably took an active role in the well-being of their students. "Has your grandmother been diagnosed with dementia?"

She nodded. "Beginning stages."

"You may want to consider hiring help of your own." He guided her outside to the sidewalk and flipped the sign on the door to closed. "From my experience, her mental state will continue to decline until she can no longer be left alone at all. Most people consider infirmaries at that point."

Miss Larson stiffened. "I will not send her away. Ever."

She would find out the difficulties soon enough. "Where have you looked?"

After hearing where her grandmother wasn't, Jesse suggested the diner. "It's quite possible she wanted coffee made by someone else's hands."

"She left the stove on. What would we have done if the house burned down?"

"Moved on like others in your situation." He smiled to take the bite from his words. "I appreciate your help with Tommy. He seemed much happier today. How was he at school?"

"The same, but I've realized that his misbehavior is a ploy to gain my attention. He seems to crave a woman's attention. Once I realized that, I came up with reasons for him to help me. He was much better after that."

She looked as if she wanted to say more.

"But?"

She sighed. "He seems overly fascinated by death. I wanted to talk with you in-depth a bit about what could grow into an obsession, but once I found my grandmother gone—"

"Thank you for your concern." Jesse took her elbow and helped her across the street. "I will speak to my son."

She nodded. "Perhaps I could send a daily report home with him each day, outlining his behavior. That way, you could address the bad and praise the good. I feel that may make him strive more for the praise."

"An excellent idea." He reached around her and opened the door to the diner.

"Grandma!" Miss Larson stopped sudden enough that Jesse plowed into the back of her.

Reaching out, he wrapped his hands around her small waist and pulled her close to keep her from falling. She felt nicer in his hands than any woman should, and he released her as if her touch seared his skin.

Without a backward glance, she rushed toward the counter where a still attractive older woman perched on a stool. "Emma, my dear. Join me for a slice of pie?" She glanced over her granddaughter's shoulder. "Who is your handsome escort?"

"Doctor Jesse Baxter, at your service." He held out his hand. "Your granddaughter has been worried about you."

"Whatever for?" She frowned.

"You weren't home, didn't leave a note, and left the stove on long enough to boil all the water out of a pan and ruin it."

Miss Larson crossed her arms and glared. Instead of looking ferocious, she simply looked more adorable than before.

"Silly me." She cast a flirtatious grin Jesse's way. "You may call me Ruth." She returned his handshake. "Thank you for going along with Emma's worries. Ever since she received a letter from my neighbor saying I'm losing my mind, she's done nothing but worry. Perhaps, I need to make an appointment to see the local doctor?"

He chuckled. "Most certainly, Miss Ruth. I look forward to it."

"For goodness sake." Miss Larson plopped on the stool next to her grandmother. "This is a dance hall, Grandma. I was worried sick."

"I'm sorry I left the stove on." Miss Ruth motioned for Jesse to sit on the stool on her other side. "Angie, pie all around, please."

"How are you going to pay for this?" Miss Larson asked. "You left your purse at home."

"I may have left my purse, but I brought a dollar."

Miss Ruth grinned. "Relax, dear. I'm not ready to be sent away quite yet."

Or any time soon from what Jesse could see. She might have occasional forgetfulness, but the woman sitting in front of him didn't seem as if she was entering into dementia at all. Instead, a zest for life sparkled from her eyes. Trim and stylishly dressed, she hadn't stopped caring about her appearance in the slightest, nor was she confused as to where she was. Miss Larson had been misled.

Still, he couldn't be too upset at the fact. Thinking her grandmother needed her, did bring Emma Larson to Oakton. For that he was grateful. He very strongly believed that the lovely schoolteacher was going to quickly become very important to the two Baxter men.

3

Grandma looked out the back door. "The pond frogs are going to be singing at the window soon."

"What does that even mean?" Emma turned from the mirror in the foyer and stared at the back of Grandma's head. "The frogs are still hibernating."

"They'll make an appearance today. A big storm is coming. It'll be here before supper."

"I'll hurry home after school." Not that Emma believed in superstition. It was 1925, after all, but she didn't want to cause her grandmother any unnecessary worry. "You stay here today, please. I'd hate for you to be caught away from home if it starts raining."

Grandma turned and nodded. "I'll need to get the laundry done and hung so it has time to dry before the storm hits."

"You do that. I love you." Emma planted a kiss on her still smooth cheek, then grabbed her school bag and lunch pail. "See you later."

Tommy and his father were waiting outside the doctor's office, just as they had every morning for the last few weeks. Walking to school had quickly become one of Emma's favorite times of the day.

The appreciative glance in Mr. Baxter's eyes caused her face to heat. It was a good thing she wasn't ill. She didn't think she could stand the embarrassment of having such a handsome man examine her. She'd rather die.

"Good morning, Doctor." She clutched her bag tighter in front of her.

"I think it's perfectly fine for you to call me Jesse by now." He grinned.

"Then, you must call me Emma. Unless we're in front of my students," she added, ruffling Tommy's hair. "Outside of school, it's all right to be called Emma in front of Tommy."

"Because I'm special?" The little boy peered up at her.

"Yes, Tommy. Very special."

"Thank you," Jesse said, "for taking an interest in my son."

His words heated her face further. Gracious. At this rate, she'd soon be as red as an apple. They needed to be on their way before she said, or did, something foolish. "He's a good boy. Are you ready for school?"

Tommy nodded.

Emma met Jesse's gaze. "My grandmother says there is a bad storm coming." She glanced at the blue sky. The day, although unseasonably warm for March eighteenth, looked perfect to her.

"I'll make sure to be on time to pick him up. You'll learn soon enough how fast the weather can change in the Ozarks in springtime."

"I'm sure I will." Emma smiled and handed her lunch pail to Tommy. He enjoyed carrying it for her, and while they still had to stop so he could examine any dead animals or lizards they found on their way, they usually made good time arriving at school and preparing for the day. This day was no different.

By midmorning, a light rain fell and gray clouds, pregnant with moisture, covered the sky. A cool breeze kicked up, keeping everyone in at recess. By lunchtime, the gentle rain had turned to a torrent.

Emma turned away from the window and the black clouds sitting on the horizon, and organized a quiet game of arithmetic baseball. If your team answered correctly, you progressed to the next base, which in this case was a designated desk.

Lightning cracked. Several children screamed. Tommy, tears streaking down his face, dove under a desk.

"We're going to die!" He covered his head with his arms.

"We are not going to die, Tommy Baxter." Emma squatted next to him. "Let's spend the next hour planning our spring recital, shall we?" She held out her hand. When he took it, she pulled him to her side. "Tell us what you've planned."

"I'm writing a letter to my mom. I'll read it in front of the audience, then put it on her tombstone."

"What an original idea." She wasn't quite sure how to respond to such a morbid contribution.

"The rain stopped," one of her older students said. "Can we go outside for ten minutes and visit the outhouse?"

Emma smiled. "My students are full of wonderful ideas today. Ten minutes. Make haste."

The floor vibrated under twenty pairs of feet. Emma followed at a slower pace. Standing on the steps of the school, she lifted her face to the emerging sun. In the distance, dark clouds announced that the rain would pay them another visit, but for now they were safe enough to take care of some business.

While they waited their turns, the younger students engaged in a game of tag. The older ones stood around and conversed with each other, the girls making eyes at the boys. Emma smiled. Oh, the adventure of school day crushes.

When the line for the girls ended, she moved from the steps to the outhouse. "Y'all wait here for me. When I come out, it's time to resume our lessons."

She returned to a heavy stillness. The cool breeze had died, and the air turned an unhealthy oppressive green. Remaining as calm as possible, she instructed the students to return to the classroom.

"Is there going to be a twister?" Ryan, one of her older students, lowered his voice. "I remember one time when the air turned green, we had a doozy of one."

"I certainly hope not." She forced a smile to her face. "Help me get the students inside, please. We don't want to start a panic."

"Do you want me to have them sit at their desks?"

"For now." Her face hurt from the effort of keeping a smile there. "Stay close by the cellar in case I need you to open it."

He nodded, his face paling and entered the building with the rest of the students. Emma remained on the steps, her gaze glued on the rapidly approaching, swirling, ink-colored clouds on the horizon.

The wind picked up again, whipping her skirt around her knees and sending a forgotten lunch pail clattering across the yard. Emma held her hair out of her face and kept her gaze on the horizon.

~

Town residents raced past the doctor's office. Jesse stepped onto the sidewalk.

"Best get to safety, Doctor," an elderly man said. "A twister was spotted about six miles from here. My son telephoned the wife and said it was headed this way. It's the biggest one he's ever seen. They don't think it's going away."

Jesse glanced at the sky overhead. The rain had stopped and the wind had died down. Other than a yellowish cast to the sky, there was nothing to signify another storm. He stepped into the street and glanced between the buildings.

His heart stopped. As far as he could see on the horizon was blackness. Another storm was coming. What if it was as bad as the old man predicted? Tommy was terrified of storms. The poor boy was scared of a lot of things since his mother died.

With everyone within sight heading home, Jesse doubted there would be a large demand for his services. Not until the storm passed at least. He should have time to fetch his son from school. They could spend some father/son time together. Something they both needed.

Did he have time to get to the school if a twister was coming? He eyed the road in front of him, then glanced back at the horizon. He had to chance it. His son needed him. He locked the door to his office and climbed behind the wheel of his Model T. It was only a mile. He should make it with no problem.

The car sat on an angle. He climbed back out. One of the tires was flat. He'd have to go on foot. He sat off at a fast pace.

The wind picked up along with his sense of urgency. He plucked his hat from his head and tucked it under his arm. "Afternoon, Willis," he greeted a neighbor passing on a bicycle.

"Doctor. Looks like the storm might pass us after all."

"I heard it's a twister." Jesse stopped and glanced between the thick trees.

"Yep, but someone said it was going to go east of us. Still, I'd best get home and see to the wife." He pedaled away.

Jesse didn't like indecision. If the approaching storm didn't contain a twister, it would still drop an awful lot of rain. It was best he take Tommy home.

He passed an open field and glanced to his left. His heart leaped to his throat. The wind ripped his hat from his hands and sent it soaring into the sky. The air filled with the sound of a rushing train as a twister that stretched as far as Jesse could see barreled toward him.

Whirling, he raced for the school. Emma fought against the wind to close the door.

"Get inside!" Jesse took the stairs two at a time and threw himself against the door. "Get the kids into the cellar."

She nodded, her eyes wide and glued to the sight over his shoulder.

"Emma!"

She rushed inside.

Jesse pulled the door closed as the first student disappeared into the hole in the floor. "Make it faster, children. Twister is coming."

Shingles were ripped from the roof and tossed across the yard like toys. The children screamed, ducking and covering their ears as the building shook.

"Open the windows, Emma." Jesse ordered the

oldest student into the cellar. "I'm tossing the little ones in. We've got to go faster."

Emma rushed around the room, throwing the windows wide. She screamed as one shattered from a flying tree limb, peppering her with glass. The limb bounced off her head before whirling back out the window. Instead of resorting to hysterics, she continued to open the windows as Jesse helped children to safety.

"Your turn, Emma." He held out a hand.

The roof ripped from the schoolhouse, taking several of the desks with it. Keeping one hand on the cellar door, Jesse stretched his arm to Emma. "Grab hold!"

She fought against the wind, finally latching onto him. He shoved her into the hole and moved to follow her. The twister yanked his feet from under him. His muscles screamed as he fought to keep his hold on the door.

Emma reached for him, along with two boys who looked to be around the age of fourteen. With a mighty tug, they pulled him inside and latched the door closed. They all moved to the far corner and huddled together as the storm raged overhead.

Jesse pulled Tommy behind him and shielded him and a couple of young girls with his body as Emma did the same with the other students. The ground shook around them as all sound except the tornado ceased to exist.

Fumbling in the dark, Jesse found Emma's hand and clutched it like a lifeline. From the stickiness of her palm, he knew she was injured. Everything in him wanted to look her over and care for her.

The cellar door banged, then stilled as something

heavy fell across it. After what seemed like hours, but was only minutes, the world outside the cellar quieted. The wind turned from a roar to a whisper. Light peeked through the boards of their shelter.

Jesse cupped Tommy's face. "Are you all right?"

"You came for me." Tears left furrows in the dirt on his son's face.

"I will always come for you. Now, I need to check the others, all right?"

"Miss Larson, are you able to do a roll call?" He fumbled in the dim light for a lantern. "I'll see if I can get the door open."

She called off names, the children answering one-by-one. Jesse found a lantern and lit the wick with matches from his pocket. His spirits lifted with the sight of light, and he unlatched the cellar door and pushed.

Nothing. He handed the lantern to Emma and pushed with his shoulder. The door didn't budge. They were trapped.

"At least we have light," she said, right before she crumpled to the floor.

4

Emma opened her eyes to see Jesse and her students staring down at her. The light of the lantern reflected in their eyes. "What happened?"

"Don't move. You fainted." Jesse pressed a hand gently against her shoulder to keep her from sitting up.

"Nonsense. I've never fainted in my life." She put a hand to her aching head. "I'm bleeding?"

"You were hit by a tree." He slid an arm under her and helped her sit. "Slowly now. How many fingers am I holding up?"

"Two." She glanced around at her students, mentally taking a head count. They were all there. Thank God. She rested her head against the dirt wall of the cellar. "Would you older boys kindly help the doctor get us out of here?"

The two boys nodded in unison and leaned against the cellar door. Jesse studied her for a moment, then apparently deciding she wasn't going to faint again, joined the boys.

They shoved their shoulders against the door. It raised an inch, then fell back into place with a bang.

Jesse scooted beside Emma. "We'll have to wait for rescue."

"There is a jug of water in the corner," she said. "No food, but surely someone will come in a short while." Ignoring the pounding in her head, she crawled to the jug. "Only sips, children. We don't have restroom facilities down here."

"Let me do that." Jesse stopped her. "You need to rest. You most likely have a concussion. I can't determine for sure until we get out of here, but it's best to let me and the older students care for the others."

It sounded good to her. Movement made her dizzy.

Had grandma fared the twister okay? If she had wandered into town and been caught in the storm, anything could have happened. Emma prayed for her grandmother's and the town's residents' safety.

Around her, the sniffles and soft crying of several of the students tore at her heart. She opened her arms and pulled a few of them close, thankful everyone was accounted for and, other than minor scrapes, unharmed. It seemed as if the school took a direct hit from the tornado. Things could have been much, much worse.

Tears fell silently down her face. Thankful for the darkness that hid her fear, she kept her gaze glued to the crack of light seeping into their prison from cracks in the wooden cellar door. As she sat, the terror of the last half hour washed over her, smothering her, stealing her breath.

Jesse's struggle not to be swept away. The window shattering, prickling her skin with glass. The tree limb bashing her in the head. The children's screams. It threatened to overwhelm her. Her breathing quickened. Her pulse beat in her head.

"Focus on my voice," Jesse said, taking her hand in his. He smoothed his thumb over the skin in a soothing manner. "Breathe with me. In. Out. In. Out. We're going to be fine, Miss Larson."

She wanted him to call her Emma. She wanted him to wrap his strong arms around her and tell her that the world outside was unchanged, undamaged. She wanted her head to stop hurting and her stomach to settle. Instead, she did as he instructed, regulated her breathing, and clapped her hands to get the attention of her students.

"Let's practice our spelling, shall we? It will pass the time until the door is unblocked."

Jesse patted her shoulder and made the rounds with the water jug as the students took turns reciting the words they had written that morning. Had it only been a few hours? The day seemed to have stretched into two while she wasn't looking.

"Take a drink," Jesse said, offering her the jug.

She shook her head. "The children need it more. I'm fine."

He sighed, his breath tickling the hair around her face. Until then, she hadn't realized how close they were forced to sit. While the cellar was intended as a storm shelter for the small school, she doubted anyone thought a six-foot tall man would also have to squeeze in.

"How is Tommy?" she asked. "I know how frightened he is. My fainting must have sent him over the edge."

"He's fine." Jesse chuckled. "I've put him in charge of looking for something to eat. I told him how important the task is."

"There's no food down here."

"I know, and forgive me for the lie, but it will keep

him distracted for a while. He needs to feel needed."

She nodded, even though he couldn't see much more than her shadow, then instructed the students from spelling to multiplication tables. Since the reciting of spelling words, the sniffling and cries had faded until she could no longer hear them. "Once we've finished with that, we'll move on to singing for our recital—shh. Listen." She stopped the students from reciting. "I think someone is here to rescue us."

A banging from above them had them all on their feet and shouting. Jesse pulled Emma to her feet and, keeping his arm securely around her waist, kept her close. He pounded on the door from their side, three quick knocks, then two more. Their cheers increased when a repeat of the pattern sounded from the other side.

"The roof fell," someone shouted. "It's going to take a while to dig you out. Sit tight."

She groped for Jesse's hand. Once she found it, she clutched it like a lifeline and watched as the light through the closed door grew brighter.

After what seemed like an eternity, the door swung open. The face of a bearded man appeared in the opening. "Anyone injured?"

"Miss Larson is," one of her students called out. "She fainted. Take her first."

Emma shook her head. "No, please, the students—"

"They won't go until you do." Jesse transferred her hand to the stranger's, and she took a step into freedom.

~

After all of the children had been taken out of the cellar, Jesse stepped into the late afternoon sunshine.

While some students hovered around Emma, others were being shepherded away by their frantic but relieved parents.

"Jesse!" Emma rushed toward him, her beautiful face streaked with dirt, tears, and tiny cuts. "Parents are taking their children willy-nilly. How will I ever keep track of who goes where? I think one of the older boys ran off on his own. Please, help me."

Jesse stuck his fingers between his lips and blew a shrill whistle. "Students over here immediately!" He grabbed a board from the ground, laid it across two battered desks, then retrieved a piece of paper stuck in a bush. "Parents, you must sign your children out before leaving with them. It is imperative that Miss Larson account for each and every one of her students."

"Thank you." Emma looked unsteady on her feet, but the brave little thing squared her shoulders and greeted the next set of parents.

He did his best to keep an eye on her while making the rounds of the people who had showed up at the school. While everything in him wanted to administer medical aid to Emma, he knew she wouldn't slow down until every last one of her students was headed home. In the meantime, he would make sure the remaining students and those who had helped rescue them were uninjured.

"Over here, Doc." A thin, wiry man slumped on a piece of the schoolhouse. "I seem to have hurt myself digging out the children."

Jesse knelt in front of the man and took what was left of his hand in his own. The flesh was torn nearly to the bone. "What happened?"

"Sybil is my little girl. The youngest." The man

shrugged. "Knowing she was buried under that wreckage, well, I didn't think of anything but digging her out. I'm not the only one hurting."

He needed his supplies. "Ryan." The oldest of Emma's students turned. "See if the gentleman with the automobile over there will give you a ride to my office." He dug the key from his pocket. "In a large metal cabinet is my black bag, some gauze, and disinfectant. I need those items immediately."

"Yes, sir." It wasn't until the boy turned to leave that Jesse saw the gash in his calf, but Ryan was in the car and headed down the road before Jesse could call him back.

While he waited, he lined up those needing his attention. He stripped off his shirt and ripped it into bandages. They weren't the cleanest, but they were better than nothing. He shivered in nothing but his undershirt.

"Can I help?" Tommy tapped his arm.

"You're just the person I need." Jesse smiled down at his very dirty, but very much alive son. "Can you get the water jug and fill it at the pump? I'm sure just about everyone here could use a drink."

"Yes, sir." A grin spread from one bruised cheek to the other, but like a little soldier, Tommy dashed off to serve others.

Some of his patients needed stitches. Most of them needed a good cleaning. None of which he could effectively do amongst the tornado's destruction. Instead of sending someone for his bag, he needed to find a way to load everyone up and transport them to his clinic.

The automobile carrying Ryan arrived half an hour

later. "Doc, there isn't anything left of your clinic," the boy said. "We gathered up what we could, and found your bag floating in Miller's pond." He grimaced. "Your automobile is flattened against a tree."

He loved that car. Still, better the car, than him. "Thank you. Have a seat so I can look at your leg." Jesse ran the fingers of both hands through his hair, then turned to the owner of the car. "Tell me."

"The town is gone, sir." The man whose stylish suit was most likely once pristine, hung in shreds on his average-built frame. "Down to the house foundations."

"Everything is gone?" He glanced to where Emma signed up the last remaining student.

"All but some of the outlying houses and the library. They're turning that into a makeshift hospital. I've been asked to bring you. That tornado was miles wide, Doc. There's a lot of injured and … well, injured people."

"I'll come, but not without these people. I've injured here, too."

"I spotted a lumber truck down the road. I can probably catch up to them. We could load everyone on the back and transport them that way." He raced away, leaving Jesse to tend to the others the best he could.

He shoved aside the feelings of loss at the destruction of his clinic. What would he tell Emma about her grandmother? Her home? He couldn't let her see the destruction without some kind of warning.

He wrapped Ryan's leg, told the boy to stay seated, then made his way to where Emma sat on a patch of grass not filled with debris from the schoolhouse. "Let me look at your head."

"I'm fine."

"You've got quite a goose egg." He sat beside her. "We're transporting everyone here to the library."

"Why not your clinic?" She raised weary eyes.

"It's gone, wiped out, along with most of the town." He took her hands in his. "I don't know for sure whether your house stands or not, but I've heard there's nothing left of Oakton but the library. You need to be prepared for the worst."

"Grandma?"

"I don't know. I'll help you at the first opportunity, but first, I need you and the others at the library so I can care for your injuries." He turned her hand over. "Your palm needs stitches. Once I take care of you, I'm going to need your help. There are going to be too many hurt people for me to do it alone."

His request was unfair. She would want nothing more than to head home and search for her grandmother. But, until Jesse was able to console her if she confronted the worst, he couldn't allow her to go.

She nodded. "Will you at least send someone to see whether my grandmother is all right?"

He stood and held out his hand. "That, I can do."

5

Emma did her best to help those loaded onto the flat bed of the logging truck, but when they hit the town line, nothing occupied her attention like the devastation in front of her. Smoke rose above Main Street from the multiple fires. Where there were once shops and homes to break up the horizon, now there was nothing but rubble.

Bedraggled people picked through the mounds of debris in search of valuables that could be salvaged. A little girl, not old enough to attend school, clutched a muddy rag doll in her hand and stared vacantly at the truck as it rumbled past.

As they passed the place where the clinic had once stood, Jesse made a strangled sound deep in his throat. Emma slipped her hand in his, not only for his comfort, but for hers.

"Look, Dad," Tommy said. "There's your filing cabinet and my toy chest. The most important things are there."

Jesse wiped a tear from his eye. "Yes, son." He pulled Tommy onto his lap. "The most important thing survived." He rested his cheek on top of his son's dirty head.

Emma looked away, not wanting to intrude on such a private moment. Instead, she gave into a moment of self-pity and fear. She wanted to ignore Jesse's request of help and dash away to see whether her grandmother was okay. Since they lived past the library, she wouldn't know until morning. Unless...

She straightened. Perhaps, Grandma was at the library helping. It would be just like her to see where she was needed. Hope sprang in her chest. Of course, that's where Grandma would be. But what if she had lost touch with reality and wandered off, only to be swept away by the twister? She needed to do something to pull her mind off such terrifying thoughts.

Pulling her hand free from Jesse's, she crawled to the other side of the truck where Ryan sat, his injured leg stretched in front of him. "We'll find your parents right away."

"We passed my house, Miss Larson. There's nothing left of it."

Her heart fell. "They're probably at the library frantic over worrying about you."

"If Pa would have been able, he would have come for me."

"Oh, sweetie." She put her arms around him, pulled his head to her chest, and let him cry. When none of his family had arrived to take him home after the twister, she had feared they might be gone. He was the only one of her students left unclaimed. "I don't know where my family is, either. We'll find them together. And, if you're able, you can go with me tomorrow to make sure the students who weren't signed out made it home all right."

He nodded and pulled away. "I'm sorry I acted like

a little kid."

She patted his arm. "You've done the work of a man today, in spite of your injury. You should be proud."

"The trees look like ghosts," he said, glancing above them, "with clothes hanging from limbs stripped of their leaves."

"Yes, they do." Especially with night falling and thickening clouds floating across the rising moon. They'd have more rain before morning. Which brought to mind Grandma's warning that morning. Emma should not have brushed her words aside. She was older and wiser and knew much more than twenty-two-year-old Emma ever could, despite her schooling.

"We're here." Jesse clapped a hand on her shoulder as the truck stopped. "I'll take care of you first, so you are more able to help me." He peered into her face. "I'll need you to assess people's injuries and put the most severe first. Can you do that?"

She nodded. "I'm not afraid of blood. Perhaps Tommy could gather the uninjured children in a corner for some games?" It would help not to have them underfoot and the grieving boy, while holding up like a real trooper had done well so far, he might not be able to handle the horror they could face inside the building.

"That's a great idea." He lifted his son to the ground. "See what you can do, son." He then helped Emma down. "Go see if your grandmother is inside. Ryan, I see someone you'll want to hug." He pointed to the stoop in front of the library.

"Mom!" Ryan limped away, dragging his injured leg. He swept his mother into his arms and wept.

Emma stopped before entering the building. "He's

been very helpful today."

His mother clasped Emma's hands. "Thank you. We couldn't come. His pa has a broken leg, and I couldn't leave the baby."

"Everyone is all right?" Ryan sagged against the building.

"The house is gone, but we're all still breathing." She caressed his cheek. "Let's take you to your pa. He's worried sick."

"The doctor will tend to both of them when he can," Emma said.

She stepped into the library, dismayed to see so many lying on the floor. Cries of pain assaulted her ears, and she wrinkled her nose against the scent of blood. It looked like any picture she'd ever seen of a battlefield. Except, these weren't soldiers and nurses. These were families; women and children.

Where did she even begin to help them?

She dug under the librarian's counter and found ribbons in red, white, and blue. Left over from a Fourth of July celebration, no doubt. While she made the rounds of the room, doling out ribbons to distinguish the severity of those needing medical attention, she asked after her grandmother, and her students. Several had taken refuge with their families in the library. She mentally scratched them off her list of students to locate.

"I saw your grandmother bringing in the laundry," one lady said, "right before the rain came. I'm not sure what happened after that. I rushed home myself. Don't you have a storm shelter?"

"No." Emma blinked back tears. No storm shelter, no house, no school, and possibly no family. She had nothing but the clothes on her back and a hand that needed tending to.

She glanced up as Jesse entered the building and made a beeline in her direction. "There are more here needing attention than I feared," he said. "Let me stitch your hand."

"I handed out ribbon. Red is the most severe, then blue, and white are only minor scrapes that people can probably take care of themselves if given clean water." She hissed as he dabbed her cut with iodine.

"Thank you."

He glanced up with eyes so weary she wanted to close them and tell him to sleep.

"I can't do this without you," he said. "How is your head?"

"It hurts, but I'll live." She glanced around them at the casualties. Many probably weren't as fortunate. What would the day's death toll be?

~

Just as he figured she would, Emma endured the stitching of her hand with little complaint, other than the occasional hiss or groan when the needle pierced her skin. He would have liked to have numbed the area, but without his supplies … While Jesse had sent more men to scour for any supplies not blown away by the tornado, and they had come back with more than he'd thought possible, he still felt inadequate to meet the overwhelming demand in front of him. He was grateful for the lovely young woman in front of him. He needed her strength.

"Try to keep it clean," he smiled. "Which will be hard in the midst of all this."

"I'll do my best. Jesse, these people need blankets,

food, and water. They need the comfort of a preacher."

"The parsonage was flattened. The pastor and his wife are missing, presumed dead."

"I'll hand out books and bibles. At least it might occupy their minds for a bit." She pushed to her feet, wincing when she put pressure on her hand. "Send for me if you need me."

He wanted to call her back. He wanted to pull her close and kiss her. It didn't matter who saw them. Feeling her lips against his, her heart beating against his chest, wrapping his hands in her hair and pressing her so close to him that she moaned ... it would remind him of what they fought for. It would be a celebration that they lived. Instead, he watched her walk away, stopping here and there to offer a word of comfort or a tender touch. The ministering angel of Oakton, Missouri.

He pushed to his feet and approached the closest red-ribboned patient. An elderly man with a strip of steel protruding from his thigh. Jesse needed a sterile operating environment, not a dusty library. He spotted a door in a nearby wall and opened it to reveal a room devoid of everything but a six-foot table and a handful of chairs.

"I need a couple of men over here," he called. He ordered them to take out the chairs and to bring in all the medical equipment he had. Jesse had found his surgery. "Does anyone know why help hasn't arrived?"

"Road is blocked in both directions," one of his helpers said. "It's going to be hours before we get any help."

Jesse sighed. "I need that man over there put on this table. Then, I need those holding red ribbons brought closer to this room. Find Miss Larson. I need a surgical nurse."

"I can help you, young man." Emma's grandmother strolled to his side. "Now that I'm out of the tree, I'm willing to help."

"From the looks of that arm, Ruth, you need medical attention yourself." The sleeve of her blouse revealed a long gash on the lower part of her arm.

"Stitch me up and set me loose." She grinned.

"Grandma?" Emma stood in the doorway, dark eyes wide. She covered her face with her hands and sobbed.

Ruth wrapped her in a hug. "I'm fine, sweetie. The house is ... relocated, and I spent some time in a tree, but I'm here and kicking. I'm very relieved to say the same of you. Now, no more tears. This handsome doctor needs our help."

Emma grinned over her shoulder. "Tommy is playing school teacher."

Jesse laughed. "You had a great idea in getting him to help. Can you act as nurse for me now?"

She nodded and stepped aside as the first patient was brought in. "Where do I wash?"

"There's iodine in that bucket. It will stain your skin and your bandages, but that can't be helped. Ruth, sit there so I can stitch you. It will take both of you to hold Mr.—" he glanced at the man with the steel in his leg.

"Connors. They don't have to hold me down, just hold my hands. You yank, then send me on my way."

"It will take a bit more than just a yank, Mr. Connors." Jesse plunged his hands into the bucket of disinfectant. "It's quite possible you nicked an artery. We must be prepared for anything."

Ruth took one of the old man's hands and Emma the other. "Now, Mr. Connors," Ruth said. "If I recall correctly, you promised me a dance at the next social."

"That I did." He smiled under his thick mustache. "You make sure the doctor saves my leg, and we'll have that dance."

Emma glanced up. Jesse pressed his lips together. "I'll save the leg. On three, ladies. One, two, three." He slid the steel from the man's thigh, tossed it in the corner and clamped a towel over the wound.

Mr. Connor grunted and passed out.

"Emma, please hold this towel in place while I get my forceps."

She rushed to hold the towel in place. Her face had paled to the color of the clean towels at the opposite end of the table, but she kept a determined look on her face.

He pulled the small utensil from his pocket, then peered under the towel Emma held. *Thank you, God.* No arterial spraying.

Patient after patient came in and out of the makeshift triage until the faces blurred together and all Jesse saw were the wounds. Supplies were running dangerously low, they still had nothing to make the survivors comfortable, and Ruth swayed on her feet.

"We've made it through the red ribbons," he said, "and most of the blue. You two go rest."

Emma shook her head. "I'll stay as long as there are patients."

"Well, I'm not as young as you." Ruth kissed her cheek. "I'm going to find me a corner to curl up in."

"Help has arrived! The Red Cross is here!" Someone shouted from outside.

Cheers rose from inside the library.

Jesse did what he'd wanted to do all day. He pulled Emma close and kissed her.

6

After a virtually sleepless night listening to the cries of those who had lost loved ones or were in physical pain, and feeling Jesse's kiss still on her lips, Emma stepped outside and breathed deeply of the moist morning air. Grandma helped a few of the other women brew coffee for the refugees and had waved across the room at Emma, reassuring her that she was fine.

The page containing the list of students who were unaccounted for crackled in her pocket. She hoped Jesse could accompany her in a few minutes, but if duty called, she would go alone. She had to know the children were safe.

Jesse, looking as if he hadn't slept a wink, joined her on the steps. "Beautiful morning." His gaze softened.

"Except for the path of destruction." The aftermath was more shocking in the bright morning light.

Entire buildings were gone or pushed off their foundations to sit a few feet from where they once sat. One house looked untouched except for the fact it had been moved several feet by a giant swirling monster.

"We're alive. That makes it beautiful."

She nodded. "I have to visit the homes of five of my students and make sure they are accounted for."

"I'll go with you. My patients are resting and won't need me for an hour or two. The Red Cross can handle anything that arises in the meantime. I'll borrow an automobile. Will you be ready in fifteen minutes?"

She nodded and watched as he entered the building. She ran her finger over her lips. Would he kiss her again or had last night been a one time occurrence brought on by the arriving Red Cross and the knowledge that everything would be fine? Would he mention the kiss or had it meant nothing to him?

She shrugged. Now was not the time to dwell on such fantasies. They had months of surviving and reconstruction ahead of them. Not to mention she wanted to resume classes as soon as possible. The children would need a semblance of normalcy in their lives.

Jesse leaped from the library steps and jogged to a waiting automobile. Emma joined him, grateful she wouldn't have to walk miles that morning. Her entire body ached, not to mention the throbbing in her hand. Still, she had managed to sleep for four hours. Something she doubted Jesse got any of.

"Where to first?" he said, climbing into the front seat.

"The Olsons. It's a brother and sister, ages ten and eight. They dashed away the moment they were pulled from the shelter."

"I'm sure they're fine."

"I agree, but I want to make sure they didn't arrive home to no parents." Her heart couldn't bear the thought of any child finding their parents dead, then staying because it was their home. "If they're alone, we'll have to bring them back with us."

"Are there other orphans?" He glanced quickly at her, then back to the road to swerve around a pile of debris.

"A few." Tears pricked her eyes. "The Red Cross is caring for them." While those left without parents weren't among her students, she still felt a responsibility toward them and wished she had the means of having them live with her. Live with her where? At the library? She shook her head. She was as homeless as the rest of the town. The orphans would be better off with a foster family somewhere else in another city.

The Olsons' two-story farmhouse still stood, missing several shingles, and the front porch sagged, but the home still sat on its foundation. Emma smiled and pushed open her door as Daisy Olson bounded down the steps.

"Teacher!" She ran to Emma and wrapped her small arms around Emma's waist.

Emma returned her hug, then squatted in front of her. "Is your family all right?"

Daisy nodded. "Robbie took me toward home real fast, and we met our parents halfway between school and here."

Mrs. Olson, a friendly, plump woman in a green house dress and faded yellow apron, made her way to them. "So nice of you to come check on my little ones." She glanced over Emma's torn and dirty dress and shook her head. "Come. I have clothes for you," she said in a thick German accent. "My sister lived with us for a time, but she is gone. She was tiny like you." She turned and bustled to the house, leaving Emma and Jesse to tag along.

Thirty minutes later, loaded down with clothing for Emma, a few things the Olson children had outgrown, and some canned food for the refugees, Emma and Jesse headed down the road to the next house on her list. The driving was slow because of a road clogged with fallen trees, boards, and household items. Emma stared at an undamaged Dutch oven sitting beside the road as if its owner had placed it there and simply walked away.

"Oh, no." She raised her head and stared at where the Roberts family had lived. The house was gone. Nothing remained but a partial rock fireplace. "Where is Daniel?"

"There." Jesse pointed to where a blanket had been hung between two saplings in front of a door in the ground. Daniel and his parents emerged from the storm cellar and waited for Emma and Jesse to approach. "It looks like they're living in the cellar. But, at least you know the boy made it home safely."

Emma nodded. "I wonder how many of the town's residents aren't even that lucky to have a sod roof." She forced a smile on her face and moved forward.

~

The Roberts family had a well-stocked cellar, and while the cellar was only a place to escape the weather, they did have a roof over their heads. Of a sorts. He would hate to have to live in such a small place underground. After making sure no one had injuries he needed to tend to, Jesse drove to the next, and last, house on Emma's list.

There was no sign of life at all. The house, knocked off its foundation, leaned against a massive magnolia tree that looked untouched by the storm. A nearby paddock, with pieces of the fence missing, was empty. If it had held livestock, they were gone. Most likely hiding in the woods.

"Stay here," he told Emma, shoving open his door. If there were casualties, he didn't want her seeing them. "Stand by the car and call for the children."

"What if they're in the house?"

"Hopefully, no one is in the house." Jesse marched across the lawn. Somewhere in the distance, a dog barked. Behind him, Emma called for a Rachel and Sarah. His heart sank. Tommy had spoken of the twin girls his age many times. The thought of them being out here alone was too much.

He ducked and peered through the shattered front window of the house. "Hello? It's Doctor Baxter and Miss Larson. Is anyone in here?"

"In here." A childish voice came from the recesses of the building. "Mama is hurt. I'm taking care of her."

"I'll go." Emma pushed past him.

"It isn't safe."

"The girls will be more comfortable with me. If something happens, go for help." She gave him a sad smile, and crawled through the window.

He grunted and followed. There was no way on earth he was letting her enter such a hazardous condition alone.

"Sarah? Rachel?" Emma's voice was almost lost in the darkness.

Had those poor children been in here since the storm yesterday? In the dark with their injured mother? He scooted back out of the window and raced for his medical bag. By the time he rejoined her, Emma was in the kitchen, kneeling next to a fallen beam that lay across a woman's legs. Two dirty children sat next to her.

"The girls found her this way. She's alive, but I think her legs are broken." Emma scooted out of his way. "The children said their father is away looking for work."

He nodded. "Mrs. Jensen? Can you open your eyes?" Jesse took her pulse, alarmed that it was dangerously low.

"We take turns giving her water and bread," one of the girls said. "That's all we could find."

"You've done a wonderful job of taking care of your mother."

Mrs. Jensen's eyes opened. "They shouldn't have run home on their own, but the little darlings wanted to make sure I was all right. They think that since my husband is in St. Louis, it is their responsibility to take care of me."

"How is your pain?"

"It's pretty high, but if you can lift the beam, I think I can scoot out from under it."

He couldn't see any other way. "Move back, girls." He glanced around until he located some bricks. "Emma, scoot these under when I lift." He planted his shoulder under the higher end of the beam and heaved.

"A little more," Emma said.

"Easier ... said ... than done." His legs trembled as he pushed upward.

"She's out." Emma scrambled to the woman's shoulders.

"I'll need to temporarily splint her legs, then it will take both of us to get her in the car." He gathered two pieces of wood the length he needed and searched the floor for twine. Instead, he found some dish towels. He used them to stabilize her legs on the boards, then joined Emma at Mrs. Jensen's shoulders.

"I'm sorry, but we're going to have to drag you out of here. I can carry you once we're outside."

"I understand." Mrs. Jensen nodded. "Girls, wait for us outside."

With wide-eyes, they scampered out.

"On three," Jesse said. "One, two, three." They lifted and dragged her through the kitchen door frame.

Once outside, Jesse scooped the woman into his arms and rushed for the car where he propped her up in the backseat. Her children scampered into the rumble seat. "I'll drive as carefully as possible," he said. "We've food and supplies at the library."

She nodded, her eyes closed.

He drove while Emma answered the woman's whispered questions about the state of the town. Bless Emma for being a conscientious teacher. If she hadn't insisted on making sure her students were accounted for, Mrs. Jensen could very easily have laid in the house until she died. How many more were there lying injured in the rubble, waiting and praying to be found?

They needed a search and rescue team formed immediately.

"What are you thinking?" Emma asked.

He told her his thoughts. "I'm organizing one immediately after I set Mrs. Jensen's legs."

"You won't be good to anyone unless you get some sleep."

"I figured of anyone, you would understand."

She sighed. "I do, but I also know how much even a few hours of sleep helped me. Tend to Mrs. Jensen, then rest. I'll get someone else to organize the team. We'll be ready for you when you wake. I'm sure there are already people out searching. Won't you be needed more as a doctor?"

She was right. His job was to tend to the injured brought in. It was going to be hard staying behind while others searched.

"You're right. I'm needed at the library."

"And, for Tommy. He needs you where he can find you easily. He comes before anything, or anyone, Jesse, even the injured."

7

Emma helped the Red Cross hand out boxes of food to those heading back to what was left of their home. Those with minor injuries, preferred tents and storm cellars to the crowded library. Not that she blamed them. She had a small room picked out for a temporary school, but the students would be packed in like pencils in a box. She wasn't sure how conducive that would be to learning.

Besides Jesse's temporary surgical room, he had also curtained off a section of the library for a medical wing. It was definitely not a peaceful building to live, or recuperate, in.

"I'll take over here," Grandma said. "The search and rescue team is heading out, and I know how much you want to be a part of that."

"Thank you." She did want to help. While it could be heartbreaking to find the body of someone who didn't make it through the storm, finding someone alive gave her purpose. Two days after the tornado, people were still trickling into the library with amazing stories of survival and devastating numbers of fatalities. Oakton was no longer a town of residents and shops. It had become a refuge for the homeless.

She removed the apron she wore over the clothes handed down from Mrs. Olson, and strode outside to where a crowd gathered. Most of the group consisted of men, but Emma made the third female willing to offer her services. Without a family of her own, she had time on her hands until she opened up school the following week.

Jesse flashed her a grin from the back of a truck as it rumbled down the road, leaving Emma to climb onto another flatbed. Within minutes they stopped at the edge of the town's main street. Groups of three searched each flattened building. If they found anything of value not destroyed in the storm, they set it aside to be claimed by their owners.

The unseasonably warm day that had caused the storm, had fled, leaving behind chilly temperatures. Spring had decided to hold off making its appearance, and Emma shivered under the thin sweater she wore. If she were cold, how much more so would anyone be lying under the wreckage?

The thought spurred her on faster, despite the bandage on her hand. She lifted and tossed whatever debris she could handle, peering under the heavier pieces while calling out to anyone who might be listening.

A faint whimper and scuffling noise came from under a large ceiling beam. A black nose and two dark eyes poked out.

"You poor thing." Emma coaxed the puppy from under the wreckage. "Are there any more of you in there?" Further searching revealed the tiny bundle of fur to be the only survivor of its mother and litter. Emma stuck it in her sweater and moved on to the next building, blinking back tears.

"Over here!" One of the men in her group waved his arms from what used to be the town's most popular diner.

Emma scrambled over loose rocks and boards to assist him. "A survivor?"

He nodded. "A twelve-year-old boy. Said he's a newcomer to town and ducked into the diner to get out of the storm."

"Where are his parents?"

The man shrugged. When they were joined by another man, the three of them hefted beams and bricks, tossing them to the side.

A boy, blue eyes peering up from a dirty face, held out his hand. "Y'all wouldn't happen to have any water, would ya?"

Emma laughed through her tears and dashed away, cradling the puppy against her chest. Of course, the boy wanted water. Praise God he was alive. Hopefully, his parents were, too, although she couldn't think of anyone looking for a boy of his age.

By the time she returned with a bucket and a dipper, the men had the boy free and sitting on top of a pile of debris. "Sip it slowly," she said. "Are you injured?" He shook his head. "I'll fetch the doctor to look you over anyway. Your injuries might be the sort we can't see. Where are your parents?"

"It's just me and Pa. He left me at the house while he went to Harrisburg to get his last paycheck. I reckon he's on his way back, after hearing about the twister and all." He handed her the dipper to refill.

Emma glanced up and met Jesse's gaze as he walked up and squatted in front of the boy. "I'd like you to come back to the library with us, son. I have a temporary clinic set up and we can get you fed and cleaned."

"I am mighty hungry." He hopped off the debris and glanced behind him. "Lost my favorite hat. It's red and black plaid, in case anyone finds it."

Emma chuckled and handed the puppy to the boy. "Would you look after him for me? Until we get back to the library?" She couldn't bear to give the little darling away for good. Grandma would enjoy a companion for when Emma was working.

"I'll take good care of her." He nuzzled the pup and climbed onto the flatbed of the truck.

"It's good to find someone alive and unharmed." Jesse stepped beside her.

"Yes, it is. As time goes by, we'll find fewer of them. To have it be a child is that much more gratifying." Emma took a deep breath. "I'd best get back to work. The days pass swiftly, and the less people who have to spend the night buried under piles of rock and wood, the better."

"Wait."

She faced him.

"I have a proposition for you."

Her heart leaped into her throat.

~

"Nothing improper, I assure you," he said, watching the color return to her face. "The railroad is donating several empty boxcars to the town. I'm receiving two of them. One for my clinic and one to live in. I thought you and Ruth might want out of the library. We could erect a small room to attach to the boxcar to give us more room." Why wasn't she answering? Was he rambling?

"You want us to live with you?" Her eyes narrowed. "What, exactly, is not improper about that?"

"Your grandmother and Tommy will be there." He ran his hands through his hair. "I'm not making myself clear. I hope you don't think I'm offering charity, because I'm not. I need help with Tommy and you've said you need help with Ruth." Not that he thought there was anything wrong with Emma's grandmother, but that wasn't the issue here. "If we all live together, both of our issues are solved."

"I need to think about it." She turned and marched away, leaving him to wonder what he had said to upset her.

"Smooth." The boy on the flatbed laughed. "You don't know much more about women than my pa does. I'm Rory, by the way."

"I suppose you know?" Jesse crossed his arms.

"Sure. It ain't hard. They needed to be treated as fragile, precious things. You can't just ask a woman to move in with you, then tell her why. You should have let her know how much you need her. Then, pop the question." He grinned. "Probably too late now."

Jesse hoped not. The thought of Emma and Ruth living indefinitely in the library gave him chills. Other than a tent or a vacant root cellar, their options were limited. He climbed onto the flatbed as the others joined him, ready to head back to town.

Without looking his way, Emma climbed on the other truck. He sighed and reached over to pet the puppy. Other than the fuzzy little thing and the smart-mouthed young man next to him, their search had come up empty. Still, two lives were better than none, and for that he was grateful.

Back at the library, Emma retrieved the puppy and Jesse took Rory with him into his examining room. Other than dirty and a bit dehydrated, the boy was healthy and whole. He sent him to get cleaned up and fed, then made the rounds of the few patients that refused to go to the hospital in St. Louis.

Mr. Connor was one of them. Jesse peeled back the bandage and grimaced at the inflamed wound. "This is getting infected. You should have gone to the hospital."

"I'm fine. Clean it out, give me some medicine, and send me on my way. I don't need a hospital. They're full of disease and sick people." He crossed his arms and glared. "All I need are some crutches so I can get out of here."

"You aren't going anywhere for a while." He cleaned the wound, applied a fresh bandage, and gave the old man an antibiotic. "Is Ruth tending to you regularly?"

"Yep. She's becoming a regular nuisance about me taking those horse pills you prescribed."

"Good." Jesse laughed and moved to the next patient. When he finished, he went in search of Tommy

"It seems as if you've put my granddaughter in a dither," Ruth said.

"I only thought to help."

"Yes, but she's quite stubborn. Excuse me." She headed away to break up a fight between two boys.

He found Tommy playing behind the library with other children. The storm seemed to have grounded him a bit, made him less obsessed with death. Or, perhaps it was Emma's ingenious idea to make his son feel needed during the aftermath.

When his wife had taken ill, Tommy had been shuffled into a corner while Jesse focused all his attention and energy on trying to make his wife well. When she died, it had almost been too late for him to salvage a relationship with his son. He was grateful to Emma for stepping into a motherly role, even as a teacher.

"Jesse." Emma rushed toward him. "Grandma has wandered off again."

"I just spoke with her."

"Well, someone saw her heading across the vacant lot. Alone. She didn't take her purse or a sweater." She sighed. "Will you help me find her?"

"Of course." He followed Emma out the backdoor and told Tommy that he would be back in a bit and not to go anywhere. "Take care of Emma's puppy, all right?"

"Yes, sir!" He beamed as Emma handed him the dog.

"Maybe you can decide on a name for me by the time we return," Emma said.

Tommy nodded and carried the puppy to his friends.

"I don't know what I'm going to do with her, Jesse." Emma marched in the direction Ruth had gone. "I'm a teacher. I have a job to do. How can I teach and babysit Grandma?"

"Perhaps you could consider hiring help?"

Her shoulders slumped. "That will take funds we don't have."

"This is why I proposed we join forces." He glanced down at her. "I can have Ruth work with me around the clinic while you're at school and you can help me with Tommy after school. We both win with this situation."

"Hello." Ruth stepped from behind a tree and winked.

What sort of game was she playing?

"You must stop wandering off," Emma said, taking her grandmother's arm. "There is plenty of work for you to do at the library. How would you feel about working with Jesse each day?"

"That sounds wonderful." Grandma clapped her hands.

Emma sighed. "We accept your offer, Jesse."

Ruth put a finger to her lips as if she and Jesse shared a secret.

8

Emma sat on the wooden stoop Jesse had built to enable easier access for her and her grandmother. She had a hard time thinking of the railroad car as home. She and Grandma had moved in the day before with donated items, a quilt salvaged from the wreckage of their house, and a few dented and chipped dishes. It would take a long time to make the place feel a smidgeon of the hominess Grandma's home had once been.

Jesse and Tommy were joining them later that evening. Grandma was giddy at the thought of cooking for more people than just her and Emma.

Emma sighed and ran her hand over the silky, freshly washed fur of the puppy, named Annie by Tommy. Now that the little thing was clean, it was clear she was a golden retriever and barely old enough to be away from her mother. Yet, the squirmy pup was a survivor, like so many of the folks milling around what used to be a growing town. Tents, hastily erected shacks made from the debris, and railroad cars lined the street in attempts to start business owners back on the path to self-sufficiency.

As she sat, a group of men moved donated medical

equipment and supplies into the railroad car designated for a clinic and what few household items could be scavenged into the one designated as living quarters. After hanging a tattered quilt as a divider to offer privacy to Emma and her grandmother, the railroad car left little room for actual living. Still, Jesse kept his promise to keep things proper. He'd even salvaged Grandma's dented stove from the wreckage of their house.

She slipped a thin rope around Annie's neck to keep the puppy from wandering off, tied the other end to the trunk of a tree, and then stood, popping the kinks from her back. In addition to helping the Red Cross, she spent her time in search and rescue, in preparing the railroad car into some semblance of a home, and in scouring for school supplies. Thankfully, the Red Cross had slates and chalk to donate. School would resume on Monday as scheduled.

Tommy and a group of older boys ran by, dragging several metal cans behind them. Tommy cast a suspiciously guilty glance over his shoulder at Emma, and kept running. What were those rascals up to? Since they were her students, she felt a modicum of responsibility for them and decided to follow.

The group disappeared into a thick stand of trees that bordered a shallow creek. Emma ducked behind a huckleberry bush and peered through the branches. One of the older boys, Rosco, took a half-grown cat from a burlap sack. Despite the poor animal's hissing and twisting to get free, the boy tied the cans to its tail and tossed the cat into the creek.

His friends hooted and hollered. Tommy, the youngest, stared from one to the other, his laughter fading. As Emma charged from her hiding place, Tommy splashed into the creek after the frantic cat.

Once she was convinced the cat's life was no longer in danger, Emma whirled to face the boys. "Rosco Miller! Your mother will hear about this for sure."

He shrugged. "It's just a stray cat."

"That is neither here nor there. That ..." she pointed to where Tommy cradled the animal, "is a living creature and deserves to be treated as such. Hasn't this town lost enough lives in that monster twister? Have you no shame?

"I expect a five-hundred word essay due Monday morning on the reasons we are to treat every living creature with respect. As for the rest of you," she glared, "I want one hundred words. If I do not have the essays in my hand at the requested time, I will have a word with the sheriff. Now, go home!" She doubted the sheriff could do anything, but the hoodlums most likely didn't know that.

With hands on her hips, she stared down at Tommy, who stuffed the poor, wet cat into the bib of his overalls. The little boy's neck and arms were covered with superficial scratches. He peered up at her from under bangs that needed cutting.

"What am I going to tell your father?" Emma took a deep breath through her nose. "I am very disappointed in you, as I'm sure your father will be."

Tears welled in his eyes and ran down his cheeks. He tried to speak, but nothing came out except sobs.

"Oh, come here." Emma held open her arms and gathered him close, being careful not to squash the mewling cat. "It's going to be fine. But, why would you do it?"

"I want to be one of the big boys." His tears dampened the collar of her blouse.

"Even when they're doing something wrong?" She patted his back and held him at arm's length. "Tommy, that type of behavior is wrong, but I do commend you for going into the cold water after the poor animal."

"I didn't know they were going to try and drown it. Can I keep him?"

"That is up to your father." She stood and held out her hand. "We must tell him, you know?"

"Yes, ma'am." Head down, he slipped his hand into hers.

They walked back to the library, Emma dreading the encounter with Jesse, and Tommy dragging his feet for the same reason, most likely. The cat in his overalls had stopped its meowing and fallen asleep. The poor thing. She would have to make sure that Jesse understood that, while Tommy was hanging with the boys he had no business spending time with, he had made the right choice in the end.

"I think," Emma said, "that instead of trying to be one of the older boys, you should concentrate on the important task I gave you."

"Yeah?" He glanced up.

"Taking care of Annie and now this fellow. A dog and a cat are great responsibilities. Annie will need exercise on a regular basis, and both will need fresh food and water every day." She gave him a stern look. "I thought you were capable enough, but now—"

"I am capable!" He squared his shoulders. "I'll show you if you'll give me another chance."

"If you're sure." She spotted Jesse heading their

way. "Now, it's time to be a man and own up to your mistake."

~

Jesse didn't think he'd seen a more beautiful sight in a long time than Emma strolling hand-in-hand with Tommy. His eyes widened when an orange tabby cat poked its head over his son's overalls.

The stressful smile Emma gave him in return to his happy one, alerted him to the fact things weren't as rosy as they seemed. "Good afternoon?"

"Possibly." Emma motioned her head at Tommy. "Your son has something to tell you."

"Can I keep the cat?" Tommy wrapped his arms around his middle.

"Tommy." Emma sighed.

"What's going on?" Jesse glanced from his son to Emma, then back to his son.

Tommy scuffed his feet in the dirt and mumbled something about following some boys and drowning a cat. "I'm sorry!"

Jesse stepped back. "Excuse me?"

"I think he needs dry clothes." Emma put her hand on Tommy's back and guided him to their tin can of a home. "Then, he'll be back out to explain in greater detail."

Jesse nodded and rubbed his hands over his face. He needed to get more sleep. In the perpetual fog he existed in since the twister, he could have sworn he heard his son say he tried to kill a cat. He wasn't made to be a single father. Children needed two parents.

He perched on a three-legged stool someone had salvaged and stared at the dark door to their home. What kind of place was a railroad car for a woman such as Emma to live in? She needed room and light, not a box. Despite the shack attached to one end, the place was small, cramped, and smelled of pickles, of all things.

"Dad?" Tommy stepped beside him.

"Yes, son."

"I followed some older boys into the woods. They tied cans to the cat's tail and tossed it in the creek. I swear I didn't know they were going to do that. I jumped in the water and rescued Mr. Whiskers. Can I keep him?"

Jesse opened and closed his mouth, glancing over Tommy's head to meet Emma's amused glance. She nodded, telling him the story was true.

"Mr. Whiskers, huh?" He ruffled his son's hair. "I suppose you can keep him, but you must promise to never do anything remotely like that again."

"I promise." He flashed a grin and dashed away, the poor cat clutched to his chest.

"It'll be a miracle if that cat survives the day." Planting his hands on his thighs, Jesse pushed to his feet. "Was I wrong in allowing him to keep the very animal he had a hand in tormenting?"

Emma shook her head and fiddled with the buttons on the frayed sweater she wore. "No, and he did what was right in the end, but I feel as if he should have some discipline for his actions in the first place."

Again, he'd failed as a father in her estimation. Did she think that because she was a teacher that she knew all there was to know about children? Not being a parent, was she really any authority on what a child needed from his or her parent?

He took a deep breath and squared his shoulders.

"While I appreciate your concern, and you have my utmost gratitude for pulling my son away from that crowd, I am his father and have the last say in what I do or do not do with him."

Her eyes widened in surprise. Her beautiful lips parted, then closed. She gave him a curt nod. "So, Dr. Baxter, I am living with you as no more than a nanny?"

"Yes."

Wrong answer. Her dark eyes hardened like flint. "Very well. I will remember that and keep my opinions to myself." She marched away, leaving him feeling very much like one of her students who had been caught sticking a toad in someone's lunch pail.

She stopped and returned, her back straight and pert little nose in the air. "I understand that my grandmother and I are living on your charity, Dr. Baxter. For that I am grateful. And, while we will be helping each other with babysitting duties as needed with my grandmother and your son, I fully intend to find our own living space at the first opportunity." She gave another nod and stormed away.

The woman could change from sweet to stormy as fast as the weather in the Ozarks. Jesse scratched his head. He didn't remember Maureen switching back and forth as quickly, or had he been too busy to notice? With him engrossed in his medical practice, and her involved in raising a young child, they didn't spend much more than the time it took to eat supper in conversation. Had he done his wife a grave injustice by being gone from home so much?

From the moment he apprenticed under Maureen's father, it had been understood the two would marry. They'd barely known each other. It wasn't until she took ill and Jesse cared for her that he actually grew to know, and love, his wife. Still, he felt as if he knew Emma far better than he had known the mother of his only child.

The aroma of chicken noodle soup drifted from the open doorway of the railroad car. Ruth did the best with what she had, but soup was quickly becoming their supper night after night.

After the tornado's destruction, patients had little to pay him with. The Red Cross had done what they could and there were talks among the town's business owners that supplies for their various businesses would begin arriving in a month. That was a long time for hungry people with few coins in their pockets. Even if the store owners managed to stock their shelves again, who would have money to buy?

He kicked at a rock. Regardless of the area's poverty, he'd continue to help where he could and take what the Red Cross offered. He could only pray it was enough to keep food in his son's mouth. What would Maureen say if Tommy went hungry?

9

"I thought the service this morning would be more of a time of rejoicing about our blessings," Pastor Richardson said. "A time to focus on what we have instead of what we've lost." Having been unburied from a neighbor's storm shelter a few days ago, he and his wife had plenty to be thankful for. "In difficult times, it often helps for us to see exactly what God is bringing out of the tragedy."

Emma squirmed on the uncomfortable wooden bench under her. Despite losing his arm as a result of being pinned under bricks for two days, the pastor kept a smile on his face and worked as tirelessly as Jesse in easing the burdens of those still living in Oakton.

She should be ashamed of herself. Instead of feeling sorry for herself that Jesse looked upon her as nothing more than a glorified babysitter, she should be thankful she was whole, healthy, and had a roof over her head. Not to mention a job. School resumed in the morning. Day-by-day, piece-by-piece, life was returning to a semblance of normalcy. Who was she to complain?

Pastor Richardson rattled a newspaper. "Written in here is the help trickling into our fair town. The *St.*

Louis-Post Dispatch and the *Chicago Tribune* have both initiated drives for donations. Because of the kind hearts of others, we are clothed and fed. Because of the strong backs of our young men and the skills from folks like Dr. Baxter, we are kept healthy and warm."

Emma snuck a peek at Jesse and Tommy sitting a row over from her and Grandma. He ducked his head at the pastor's words.

"Tomorrow, school resumes in Oakton because of the desire of Miss Larson to make sure our children are educated. We are blessed, people. Do not forget that, no matter how hard you may be struggling."

Emma's face heated. Teaching was what she did. It was as essential to her as breathing. She didn't need accolades for doing something as important to her as it was to others.

The rustling of clothes and murmurs of conversation alerted her to the fact church had ended. She took Grandma's arm and helped her to her feet.

"That man has a way with words," Grandma said. "Did you know his wife, Delores, hasn't been the same in the head," she tapped her temple with her forefinger, "since the storm? No, I'm sure you didn't. Do you know why? Because they put on a brave face. Yep. It's a shame about Delores."

Glancing over her shoulder to where the Richardsons greeted those in attendance, Emma ushered Grandma home before she could say something embarrassing. While she had a good heart, she sometimes didn't filter the words that came out of her mouth.

"Of course, if I were locked in the dark with things crushing me for two days, I might be a bit tetched in the head, too." Grandma clutched her favorite pocketbook. To her joy, the twister had not ripped it from her hands while putting her in a tree.

"Shh." She opened the door to the railroad car and ushered Grandma inside. "You musn't say things like that where others can hear." The small coal-burning stove in the corner kept the car warm enough, Emma was able to shed her sweater.

"I was speaking to your ears only."

"Then wait until we're behind closed doors."

Grandma frowned. "When did you become such an old woman?" She shook her head, set her pocketbook on a shelf, and moved to the cooking stove. "I managed to procure a roast for today's supper. What a treat!"

She should ask how Grandma managed to get her hands on something so rare, but decided not to set her off on a tangent. Not when Emma had questions that needed answering. "Do you really think I act like an old woman?" She sat on one of the mismatched dining chairs.

"Of course." Grandma faced her. "When was the last time you had any fun?" She waved a wooden spoon at her. "I mean before the twister."

"The spring recital for the students is fun." Emma picked at a spot on the table.

"That is part of your job. That is not fun. Now, go outside and play."

Not sure how to respond to such an outlandish order, Emma stood and grabbed her sweater. "What do you propose I do?"

"Take Annie for a walk, skip, run, I don't care. Just lighten up." Grandma turned back to the stove, dismissing her as if she was a child.

Emma called to the puppy and hooked a leash to the collar Jesse had fashioned from a strip of leather. "I guess it's just you and me, girl. Somewhere we're supposed to find some fun."

They stepped into the spring afternoon. Emma watched for a few minutes as a group of men moved the benches the town had used for church. Then, she transferred her attention to a lumber truck rumbling down the street. Reconstruction would begin soon.

A few families milled around the green area in front of the library, clearly enjoying a day that promised the arrival of spring. It seemed as if everyone had a way to enjoy the day except her. Had she forgotten how to have fun? Perhaps a book from the library would help her wile away the day in a guilty pleasure. But, she had lesson plans to finalize, and she should help Grandma with the cooking. Not to mention she had mending to— no, she was ordered to have fun so fun she would find.

"Where should we look, Annie?" Tears pricked Emma's eyelids. With schooling and caring for her grandmother, she had forgotten how to do anything but work. It was useless. She'd walk the puppy for a moment, then see how she could help the patients still recuperating in a section of the library. Fun wasn't for her.

~

"Dad, there's Miss Larson." Tommy tugged on Jesse's hand. "Let's ask her to go with us."

Despite living under the same roof, Jesse and Emma rarely spoke since her assumption that he didn't value her opinion. He wanted to apologize, really, but had no idea how to broach the subject. "I doubt she'll come, but you can ask."

Tommy called out to her, and she turned. No matter the time or day, her wholesome beauty never failed to take Jesse's breath away. Today, her dark hair was pinned up under a straw hat. She wore a black and white tweed dress with a brown sweater. Not fashionable, a hand-me-down, most likely, and still she was the prettiest girl in Oakton. He held his breath waiting for her answer.

"Where are you going?" She smiled at Tommy.

"Skipping rocks at the creek. Annie can play there, too. We might even go wading."

She cut a quick glance at Jesse. He nodded. "Please come. It will mean a lot to Tommy."

"The two of you don't want to spend some time alone?"

Tommy glanced at Jesse. "No, ma'am. Not unless it's with you."

"Then I'd be delighted." She stepped into place beside them. "I've never skipped rocks before."

"Dad can teach you. He's good at everything."

Jesse shrugged at Emma's questioning look. "It isn't hard. It's all in the wrist."

"Today must be 'celebrate Doctor Jesse Baxter day'," she said. "First the pastor, now Tommy Why, if the town isn't careful, your head will grow so big you won't fit inside the railroad car."

He wasn't sure if she were teasing or whether she believed in what she said. So, to keep the peace between them, he kept his mouth shut.

When they reached the creek, he removed his shoes and socks, rolled up his pants leg, and searched for the perfect flat rocks to skip. Tommy did the same, while Emma perched on a boulder and watched. She had released the puppy's leash and the rambunctious cutie pranced at the water's edge. They made the idyllic family picture. Jesse's heart hitched at the sight.

"Come on, Miss Larson." Tommy tugged at her hands. "It's no fun just sitting there."

"Why is everyone fixated on having fun?" She scowled. "I do know how, you know."

"No one said you didn't." Jesse cocked his head. Someone had gotten her dander up. Perhaps it wasn't a good idea to have her join them. While he looked forward to her company, most days, he didn't want a sour mood spoiling a perfectly good day.

"Show me how to do this." She held out her hand.

Jesse grinned and turned her back to him. He'd show her all right, and loosen her up at the same time. He slid his hand down her arm, relishing in the feel of her trembling. He turned her hand palm side up and set a stone in the center. "It's all in the wrist."

"Must you breathe down my neck to teach me?"

"It helps." He leaned closer, watching the small hairs on the back of her neck move with each breath he took. "Try it like this." He flicked her wrist.

"I did it." She jumped and turned so fast that the top of her head smacked his nose.

Tears sprang to his eyes. He grabbed his nose and turned away so she wouldn't think he cried.

"I'm so sorry." Emma snorted, drawing his attention back to her.

"Are you laughing?" His voice sounded nasally through his damaged nose.

"No." She giggled. "I don't mean to, but you shouldn't have held me so close. It wasn't proper."

After determining his nose wasn't broken, he

narrowed his eyes and plucked her hat from her head. "Laughing at a man's distress warrants a punishment. What do you say, Tommy?"

"Dunk her, Dad!"

She shook her head. "You wouldn't dare."

"You laughed when my nose could very well have been broken." He cocked his head. "I don't think you have a say in the matter."

She jumped out of his reach.

He lunged forward.

Shrieking, she dashed around a tree. Jesse followed, wrapping his arms around her waist and carrying her to the water.

"My shoes!" She kicked, sending them flying into the grass. "Please, don't. Oh!"

He carried her into the frigid creek and dropped her. It wasn't deeper than her waist and she landed on her feet. He gave her a crooked grin and scooped water into his hands.

"No." She gave him a stern look and pointed her finger at his face. "I demand you stop it, right now."

"Do it, Dad! She isn't your teacher. She can't tell you what to do." Tommy clapped and jumped into the water. He splashed forward, ramming into Jesse.

Jesse lost his footing and fell forward. Wrapping his arms around Emma, he took her under with him. He wasn't sure whether it was the cold water or the feel of her softness that made it difficult to breathe. Maybe both.

She kicked out. Her foot caught him in the groin. He gasped, swallowing water, and released her. When he got to his feet and was able to stand without groaning, she reached out a hand.

"Truce?"

"Yes, in a minute." He took several deep breaths against the pain, then took her hand. "I think we'll stick to something mild, like skipping rocks. Pulling pranks on you can leave a man infertile."

"Oh." She covered her face with her hands and turned away. Despite acting shocked, her shoulders shook with silent laughter. The minx. She faced him, her face red. "Thank you."

"For allowing you to beat me up?"

"No." Her face softened. "For showing me how to have fun again. It's been a long time." She bent and planted a kiss on his cheek. "Let's head home. I'm sure Grandma has supper finished." She plopped her hat back on her head, retrieved Annie, and set off toward town with her dress dripping and the hand holding the leash swinging back and forth.

Jesse chuckled. What a woman. He couldn't wait to see what the future held between them. And they would have a future. He'd make sure of it.

10

The schoolhouse bell had survived the storm with only a minor dent and now stood proudly next to the Oakton library. Emma reached up to ring it, signaling the end of recess, when a fancy tan car stopped in front of her.

A handsome man in a pin-striped suit exited and smiled up at her. "My name is Jonah Spencer. I'm trying to locate the person in charge of Oakton, or what's left of it."

"That would be Mayor Blackwell. He's in St. Louis for the week."

"Are you the librarian?" He placed his foot, encased in a shiny, polished shoe, on the bottom step.

"Schoolteacher." She glance over his shoulder to where her students watched with wide eyes. "I really must bring them in for their studies."

"My apologies. It doesn't do to stand in the way of education." He flashed a grin, his teeth startingly white in his tanned face. He turned and surveyed the area. "I don't suppose there is a place to rent a room?"

"There isn't much left after the twister, but Mae Jennings, who lives two miles down the road, might have a room. Her's is one of the few houses still standing and occasionally lets one out for reconstruction workers. It's not fancy, but it's clean."

"Good to hear." He glanced back at his car. "I hope she has more than one room. Thank you, Miss?"

"Larson." She rang the bell and ushered the children inside before Mr. Spencer could take up more of their day. With one last look over her shoulder, she watched as he slid into the driver's seat of the swanky automobile and drove away.

What could such a fancy man want with their little town? She shrugged. It didn't concern her. His business was with the mayor.

"Tommy Baxter, stop pulling Sally's hair and sit down. The rest of you pull out your slates. We will begin our spelling quiz." Starting school back after the disaster that had befallen the town was as bad as gaining control on the first day after summer break. Full of energy, the students squirmed, talked, and picked at each other until Emma wanted to scream.

"Once we've finished our quiz, we can work on our recital," she said. "But not before." She gave her sternest look and picked up the paper from her desk with the words. "For our first graders …"

By the time she dismissed the students, her head pounded. Not that she blamed them, but with the twister and rebuilding, no one had worked at all on their recital material. "Let's get home, Tommy." She made sure their corner of the library was clean and straightened, then led Tommy into the spring sunshine.

"That stranger is parked outside Dad's clinic," Tommy said.

"Don't point." She pushed his hand down.

"Let's go see what he wants." He dashed away,

narrowly escaping being run over by a truck.

Emma sighed and followed him. It would be a miracle if the child survived to adulthood. It became clearer with each passing day why Jesse needed her help in keeping an eye on his son. Well, that worked both ways. Grandma helped keep the clinic clean until Emma got home, and then they worked as a group to watch Tommy. Sometimes, Emma thought they could use another person or two to keep the child out of danger.

Tommy shoved the clinic door open with both hands. A woman screamed. Emma rushed forward.

A stylishly dressed woman with a bobbed hairstyle sat on the floor, her ankle cradled in Jesse's hand. "I don't think it's broken," he said. "Just sprained." He glowered at his son, who retreated sheepishly to the corner.

Mr. Spencer swept the woman into his arms and sat her on the examining table. "My sister will be fine."

"Speak for yourself, Jonah." The woman's high-pitched voice echoed in the railroad car. "I'm injured. That child is a nuisance. Why isn't he in school?"

"School is dismissed for the day." Emma inhaled sharply. "It was an unfortunate accident. One I'm sure will not happen again." How dare the woman talk about Tommy that way? If there were a window in the door, this would not have happened. It could have been anyone coming in and knocking into the woman.

She waved an elegant hand as if to shoo away Emma's words. "Please, Doctor, give me something for the pain and send us on our way. I'd like to rent a room and have a meal before night falls across this cursed mountain."

Emma gasped. What a rude, hateful person.

Instead of being offended, Jesse grinned. "I'll have you fixed up in no time."

The woman toyed with his tie. "You should join us for dinner."

"Would his son be invited?" Emma motioned her head toward Tommy.

The woman pouted. "I'm sorry. I wasn't aware the handsome doctor was married."

"Widower." Jesse bent over her ankle.

"Pay my sister no mind, Miss Larson." Mr. Spencer leaned against the wall. "Marilyn is spoiled and rude. It isn't her fault. Our parents indulged her every whim."

"Stop it, Jonah."

Jesse secured the bandage around her ankle. "There you go, Miss Spencer. I've a pair of crutches you may borrow during your visit."

"No, thank you. I've never been able to master those atrocities." She batted her eyelashes. "Would you be so kind as to carry me to our automobile?"

His eyes widened. "Of course." He scooped her up and left the clinic. Jonah shrugged in Emma's direction and followed.

Emma watched with open mouth. He hadn't thought twice about fulfilling her silly request. Hopefully, he would return soon. She could use one of the headache powders he gave to Miss Spencer.

"If that woman is going to be my new mom," Tommy said with a scowl, "I'll run away."

~

Jesse froze outside the door at his son's words. Whatever possessed him to think Jesse would marry a woman like Marilyn Spencer? Especially not after one meeting. He shuddered and stepped into the clinic. "I need to have someone cut a window in that door."

"May I have a powder?" Emma asked. "Or should I simper and bat my lashes first?"

He chuckled. "None of that is necessary." He opened his medicine cabinet and pulled out a packet of the powder. He dumped it into a glass, added water, stirred, and then handed it to Emma.

"Thank you." She tilted her head back and downed the medicine.

"Tough day?"

She shrugged. "It always is when the students have been out of school for more than a couple of days. Do you know why the Spencers are in Oakton?"

"Looking to purchase some land, is what they said." Jesse locked the medicine cabinet. "I wished them luck. People around here tend to hold tight to what they own. I think Mr. Spencer is hoping to grab the land cheap because of the twister."

"He's here to benefit from the disaster?"

"I don't know. Miss Spencer had a headache so they paid me a visit. You now know as much as I do." He ruffled Tommy's hair, then pulled him close for a hug. "Smile, son, it was an accident. You barely nicked her."

"She was mean." He raised eyes, bright green like his mother's. "You hugged her. Are you going to marry her?"

"I only helped her to her car. I don't plan on marrying anyone anytime soon" Thank goodness no one else had seen him. The last thing he needed was to spend time dispelling rumors. Ever since Maureen's death, the town had tried to find him another wife. The twister slowed down their attempts at matchmaking, but to see him with a strange woman in his arms would only refuel the fire. He stiffened. What must they think of his sharing a railroad car with Emma and Ruth?

"Where is my grandmother?" Emma stood, setting her glass on the desk.

"She left half an hour ago. Said she needed to get supper started." Jesse prayed that's where she had gone. While he had yet to see any semblance of Ruth being prone to memory lapses, he didn't want it to be on his watch if she did.

"I'll go check on her. Is it all right if Tommy stays with you?"

"Yes. I'll send him along if a patient comes in." He watched her go, the hem of the yellow dress she wore fluttering around her calves like flickers of sunshine. He smiled. If it wasn't such a crazy thought to have, he would have thought her jealous of the snooty Miss Spencer.

The thought sent a rush of warmth through him. The thought of Emma being jealous because of his attention toward another woman made his day all the more brighter. Perhaps she wasn't as immune to him as she pretended to be. Especially since she'd done everything in her power not to be in his company for more than fifteen minutes since their dunking yesterday.

He gave her credit for finding ways to avoid him with them living in such close proximity together. At mealtimes, she ate quickly, finding some reason to leave their abode, only to retire to her sleeping corner immediately upon arriving back home. He suspected she spent most of her waking time at the library. With most of his patients healing and heading home, and school occupying Emma during the day, Jesse could no longer use checking on his patients as an excuse to see her. He needed to come up with another plan.

He wondered how long the Spencers would be in town. Jealousy might be the incentive the lovely Emma needed in order to spend time with him.

While Tommy worked on copying arithmetic problems on his slate, Jesse did an inventory of his supplies, grateful that the Red Cross saw the need in having the local doctor well-stocked. By the time he finished, it was time for supper.

"Hungry, champ?" He clapped Tommy on the shoulder.

"I'm always hungry."

He chuckled. "Yes, you are." He waited while Tommy put away his school supplies, then they walked the few feet from the clinic to their home.

Emma sat on the stoop and tossed a small ball for Annie to chase. The puppy ran after the ball only to have Mr. Whiskers tackle her and steal the toy. Emma's laugh rang out, sounding as sweet as music to Jesse's ears.

He couldn't say that he loved her; it was much too soon to think that way. But, he enjoyed her company, the sound of her voice, and their bouts of sparring. She was a sweet balm to the lonely soul of a single father. He prayed it wasn't wrong of him to hope another man didn't come along any time soon to steal her away.

As if his thoughts conjured him up, Jonah Spencer pulled up in his car. He scooped Annie into his arms and handed the puppy to Emma. "Since I'm new to these parts, I was hoping you would have dinner with me. Show me around."

"I'm afraid I will have to pass on your invitation," Emma said, taking the puppy. "I have an elderly grandmother who needs me. If you're looking for a place to purchase a meal, other than the boarding house, you can try Dillon's. It's the third street car over." She smiled and entered their home.

Jesse's heart, which had sunk to his gut when Spencer offered the dinner invitation, now sprang back to his chest. It wasn't only Jesse's attentions that Emma cast aside. She wasn't accepting the attentions of any man. He could breathe easier.

11

Spring had arrived in Oakton, and it was a glorious Saturday. Since Grandma's declaration that Emma didn't know how to have fun, she had taken to walking Annie every morning and late afternoon. But, she steered clear of the creek. While it had been a fun, and confusing, afternoon, Emma didn't want a repeat of that day. Her emotions concerning Jesse were muddled enough.

"Come, Annie." She gave a gentle tug to the leash. The puppy was growing like a weed and gamboled around Emma's ankles with genuine joy in her button eyes. Emma chuckled and commanded her to walk. The puppy fell obediently into step with her, sometimes tripping over her large paws. Once she grew into them, she was going to be a big dog.

Spotting Jonah Spencer strolling in their direction, Emma ducked behind the line of shacks and railroad cars. Every day for the past week the man had made a point to stop by her home and engage her in conversation. If she were on the lookout for a suitor, it wouldn't be a dandy, self-absorbed man like him.

"What are you doing?" Jesse spoke through the open back door of his clinic.

"Taking a walk."

"It looks like you're hiding." He jumped from the car. "Who are you hiding from?"

"Jonah Spencer. Happy?"

He leaned back against the car's siding, grinned and crossed his arms and ankles. "Very."

Her face heated. "I don't see why."

"It's a gorgeous day and the view is beautiful." His gaze roamed over her, telling her which view he spoke about. And, it wasn't the mountain rising in the distance.

"You're as big of a flirt as Jonah." She marched away before he could see the smile on her face. Jesse Baxter was the type of man she would want showering her with attention if she had the time, and inclination, for romance. For now, she needed to focus on her job and on caring for Grandma. There would be plenty of time to think of romance in a few years. Twenty-two wasn't an old maid yet.

"Hello, doll!" Jonah leaped around the corner.

Emma shrieked, then stomped her foot, not only upset at his frightening her, but on the fact she allowed herself to get distracted enough for him to get close. "That was very rude." She lifted her chin and made a move to scoot past him.

He shot out his arm and blocked her between himself and the railroad car.

His aftershave tickled her nose.

"Have lunch with me."

She sighed. "Why? We have absolutely nothing in common. I'm only a country girl you've set your sights on in order to relieve your boredom."

He gave her a crooked smile. "Perhaps. But,

perhaps it's more. I find you attractive, Miss Larson."

"Thank you, but I'm not interested." She ducked under his arm and marched away.

"I tend to get my way," he called after her.

Not this time. She needed to take more care to avoid him in the future.

She glanced behind her to see Jesse watching from his clinic a few cars away, his expression grave. Jonah saluted her and melted into the shadows between the cars. It was no longer safe to wander the streets of Oakton without being accosted by unwelcome advances. She should stick to reading at the library.

She stepped back in front of the cars. Stacks of lumber in front of vacant lots showed the promise of businesses returning to full capacity someday. For now, some operated on a smaller scale than before, selling their products from tents, shacks, and donated railroad cars. If one pretended the buildings still stood, it was almost as if nothing changed.

Children ran up and down the street. Horns honked. Women browsed tables set up to display wares. What a monster storm tried to take away, the people and God fought to keep. She'd never been prouder to have moved to Oakton to help Grandma.

"My brother seems to have his eye on you." Marilyn Spencer sat in a wooden chair in front of the mayor's office, a floppy hat shading her face. She studied her nails, buffed to a high sheen. "I hope you realize you're nothing but a plaything to him." She raised a cold gaze to Emma. "A man of his wealth could never be serious about a mere schoolteacher."

"I don't think you need worry, Miss Spencer." Emma forced a smile. "I'm not searching for a husband."

She laughed, exposing a throat so white, Emma doubted it ever saw the sun. "I would hope not. Jonah is not the marrying kind, my dear. No, he prefers to use a woman until he no longer wants her. Then, he pays her off and moves on to the next."

"Thank you for the warning, but it isn't needed." Emma tugged at Annie's leash and continued her walk. Gracious, what sort of people had come to Oakton? She prayed they wouldn't stay long. They'd been there a week. That was long enough in her opinion. Especially if the brother and sister insisted on infringing on Emma's life.

She was perfectly satisfied with the way things were. She caught a glimpse of Jesse sweeping his stoop. Mostly satisfied—most of the time, that is.

~

Jesse wouldn't have thought sweet Emma to be interested in the type of lifestyle the Spencers enjoyed, but after seeing her in close proximity with Jonah, and talking with Marilyn, he wasn't so sure. What if her coming to Oakton had never been her long term plan, but a temporary one for as long as it took for her to care for Ruth?

If so, it wouldn't do him any good to look at her as more than a friend. He and Tommy needed someone willing to stay. The people of Oakton needed him. He'd been their doctor since he'd graduated from medical school. He had no plans on leaving them in the hands of someone else.

Heart heavy, he glanced at the vacant lot across the street for a glimpse of Tommy. He'd told him he could play ball with some of his friends. His son was nowhere in sight. Neither was Ruth, for that matter. She'd informed him she needed potatoes for their supper and headed a few cars down to a hastily erected building used as a store.

Sighing, he propped his broom against the clinic wall and set off at a quick pace for the store. "Afternoon, Fred," he said, greeting the owner. "Seen my son or Mrs. Larson?"

"Ruth was in here about an hour ago, then left. She didn't say where. Your boy was in earlier than that, bought a soda, then skedaddled out of here with a group of rowdy boys." He shook his head as he wiped down a table. "A bunch of troublemakers, if you ask me. They said something about doing an autopsy."

For Pete's sake. Jesse hurried back outside. He was going to tan Tommy's hide when he found him. No, he had yet to strike his son in anger, but if he were to start, that day might be the day. What was he going to do with his son?

He stood on the sidewalk and glanced up and down the street. Emma was returning from her walk, carrying the puppy now. He smiled at the sight of her struggling to hold a squirming animal that was half her size. He headed in her direction.

"Let me take her." He took Annie. "I've lost track of my son and Ruth."

She frowned. "Are they together?"

"I doubt it. Fred Harper said something about Tommy and some boys doing an autopsy."

She covered her mouth with her hand. "Goodness. Let me put the puppy away, and I'll help you search."

He followed her home, then shifted from foot-to-foot, until she returned from dashing inside. "I have no clue where to start."

"The creek is where I found the boys before."

"And Ruth?"

A shadow passed over her face. "We need to find Tommy first. Grandma is an adult. I'll pray she is only visiting a friend."

"I'm sorry." He took her elbow and helped her over a patch of uneven ground. "I know you rely on me to watch her during the day, but—"

"Only while I'm working." She slid her arm free of his grasp. "You are not responsible on the weekend."

Despite her kind words, he did feel responsible. After all, Ruth had left the clinic to go shopping. If something happened to Tommy or to her, he'd never forgive himself.

Emma patted his arm. "There is no need to fret right now. Plenty of time later if we don't find them."

"Is that the schoolteacher speaking?"

She smiled. "No, it's a friend."

"There's Ruth." Jesse motioned to where she exited a thick stand of trees, a cardboard box in her hand, and Tommy shuffling along behind her. "It looks as if my son was caught doing something wrong."

"It takes an army to keep track of him." She rushed forward. "What happened?"

Ruth gave Tommy a stern glance, then handed the box to Jesse. "I think his father can handle things from here. You remember what I said, young man." She waved her finger in front of his face. "The friends you choose now have significance on what type of man you will be in the future." She patted his head, then slipped her arm through Emma's. "Let's head home and cook supper, shall we?"

Emma glanced over her shoulder as Ruth pulled her away, clearly wanting to know what was in the box. Jesse was almost afraid to look.

"Should I wait to open this after we get home?" Jesse asked.

Tommy shook his head. "I don't think you want it in the house. It's starting to smell."

Jesse unfolded the flap. "Why is there a dead, decaying rabbit in this box? And why is its heart outside of its body?" His stomach rolled at the smell of decay, and he closed the box.

"It was already dead when I found it." Tommy shrugged, his hands wide, as if to say "what's the big deal?"

"Then, why—"

"The boys and I wanted to do an autopsy. We wanted to see what its guts looked like." He flashed a grin, the freckles across his nose crinkling. "I want to be a doctor, like you. It's never too early to start."

What could Jesse say to that? It was obvious his son had an obsession with death, and thankfully he wasn't cutting open freshly killed animals. "This is not healthy, son. You can catch diseases."

"But, I'm curious."

"Then, I'll order you a frog the schools use for biology. It can be something we do together." The thought still disturbed him, but at least Tommy would be cutting under supervision. "Let's hurry home and wash your hands. Then, I'll bury this poor thing."

He sent Tommy inside and headed to the vacant lot on the outskirts of town with a shovel and the box. Just as he finished digging the grave, Emma joined him.

"Grandma told me." She stared into the hole.

"What are you going to do with Tommy's obsession with death?"

"Find him a mother, I guess."

12

Surely, that wasn't his attempt at a marriage proposal? The look in his eyes signified that it could possibly be what she wasn't ready to think about.

Since she wasn't exactly sure what Jesse was getting at, Emma chose to remain silent and change the subject. "Grandma has beef again for supper. Do you have any idea where she is getting such prime pieces of meat?"

He leaned on the shovel. "Have you asked her?"

"I'm not sure how to without hurting her feelings. What if she thinks I'm accusing her of keeping secrets?"

He shrugged. "The only way it's a secret is if she doesn't answer truthfully when asked." He patted the dirt flat with the head of the shovel until it matched the rest of the ground. "Ready to head back?"

Grandma had the biggest heart of anyone Emma knew, and perhaps, Emma should have asked her before now where the meat came from. Instead, the moment they sat down, she blurted it out. "Where do you keep getting this beef?"

"Mr. Carson." Grandma ducked her head. "We've been spending time together since the storm. He does raise the best beef cattle."

Emma dropped her fork. The clatter of it against the china plate echoed. "Why did I not know this?"

Jesse tried to hide a smile behind his water glass. When Emma glared his way, he lost the battle and grinned, straightening in his chair. Obviously, he thought the situation quite funny.

"Sweetie." Grandma cut into her steak. "If you want to know something, all you have to do is ask."

Emma narrowed her eyes at Jesse, whose grin widened. Oh, how that man liked to be proven right.

How could Grandma be courting? She could barely keep track of herself. Isn't that why Emma was summoned to Oakton? So she could watch over her grandmother? Not that she minded. After the death of her parents in a car accident a few years before, she had been lonely in St. Louis, despite her class of students, and the occasional gentleman caller. One of them had held a special place in her heart for a while. Until his heart strayed.

She shrugged. That was in the past. Caring for Grandma gave her purpose. She hadn't thought twice about coming. Now, she second-guessed whether she had what it took to keep her grandmother safe.

"I'm asking now. Does Mr. Carson not have family of his own that needs the meat?"

"Nope. His wife is deceased. They never had any children." Grandma continued with her meal as if she couldn't see the turmoil Emma went through.

Her heart stopped. What if Grandma was to marry again and leave Emma alone? She shook away the selfish thought and cast another look at Jesse. If Grandma married, that left Emma free to decide what she wanted to do with the rest of her life. Was she ready?

"I get the impression you aren't pleased that I have a gentleman friend," Grandma said, tilting her head.

"No, I mean, yes." Emma sighed and picked at her food. "Is it serious?"

"We're just enjoying each other's company."

"This is a private conversation," Jesse said, standing and picking up his plate. "Tommy, let's take our food outside and let the ladies talk."

"Nonsense." Grandma motioned for him to sit down. "We're all family, and as far as I'm concerned, there is nothing more to discuss. I am a grown woman, and perfectly capable of making my own decisions."

"You asked me to come live with you." Tears sprang to Emma's eyes.

"Yes, because we were both alone, not because I needed a mother." Grandma patted her cheek. "Eat. Don't waste Mr. Carson's cow."

Supper sat like a rock in Emma's stomach. All along, she had thought Grandma needed her, only to realize the need wasn't as great as she'd thought. She shoved her plate aside.

There wasn't any sign of confusion in her grandmother's eyes at that moment, but what would Mr. Carson do if Grandma had one of her forgetful spells? Could he cope with her wandering off? Or would Emma be responsible for two elderly people?

She excused herself from the table and carried her plate to the small metal tub they used as a sink. Behind her, Jesse and Grandma talked more about her friendship with Mr. Carson. With each mention of his name and the way Grandma's voice softened, Emma's heart sank. It was only a matter of time before she was alone again.

She continued to clear the table, working around the other three. When she'd finished, she snapped her fingers for the puppy and clicked the leash on her collar. Maybe a walk would help her sort out her feelings.

"Don't stray far," Grandma said. She pointed her fork at Emma. "Storm is coming."

The day had been sunny and warm with no trace of clouds. How did she come up with her weather predictions?

"My bursitis is acting up. Mark my words."

Emma nodded and motioned for Annie to follow her outside. She glanced at the sky. Still cloudless. Grandma was a character. The more time Emma spent with her, the less she thought her grandmother needed her. Perhaps Grandma's invitation to come take care of her was more a cry for company than because she was losing her mind.

Load lightened, Emma picked up her pace, Annie galloping beside her. It might be time for Emma to think of her own future. One that included a husband and a family.

The wind increased. A dust devil danced in the middle of the street. A lone cloud overhead released a few raindrops, sending Emma scurrying for the nearest overhang. She really shouldn't discount Grandma's weather predictions so quickly. Having grown up in Missouri, Emma knew the weather could change in the blink of an eye.

The rain continued to fall, filling the vacant lots with mud, then stopped as suddenly as it had begun.

"Looks like you're going to get dirty, little girl," she told the dog. "You're getting too heavy for me to carry and Jesse isn't around to take you from me." She stepped from under the awning and turned toward home.

Her gaze moved between two buildings and glued to the dark cloud racing toward her.

~

"Get Tommy. We have to head to the nearest storm shelter." Jesse told Ruth as he jumped from the railroad car. Where was Emma? He swooped his son into his arms, grabbed Ruth's hand, and sprinted for the library. *Watch over her, God.*

"My granddaughter." Ruth tried to pull away.

Jesse held tight. "Once you and Tommy are safe, I'll look for her." He glanced over his shoulder as the clouds swirled overhead.

At the library, folks were crowding into the basement. Worried mothers soothed their terrified children. It was too soon. The town wasn't ready for another big storm.

Jesse thrust Tommy into Ruth's arms. "Watch over him."

She nodded.

While it was quite possible that a twister wouldn't hit their town again, he couldn't take that chance. Not with Emma on a walk somewhere, unprotected.

Jonah and Marilyn ran toward him. Marilyn clutched his arm. "Stay with me, Doctor. I'm frightened."

Jesse yanked free. "Get underground."

"There she is!" Tommy pulled away from Ruth and raced up the basement steps. The wind buffeted him, knocking him to the ground. "Miss Larson!"

Jesse grabbed him, pushed him back into the basement and rushed to help Emma. The frightened puppy strained at its leash, trying to go anywhere but where Emma wanted.

Broken tree branches whirled around them. Jesse's heart lodged in his throat as Emma was knocked to her knees by the force of the wind. She folded her arms over her head. Not again. He might not be close enough to save her this time.

He fought the wind until he reached her side. "I've got you."

"Annie."

"I've got her, too." He looped the leash around his wrist. The wind crashed overhead. Jesse bent, covering Emma with his body.

As violently as the wind had struck, it stopped with a gentle whisper, returning the world to peace. Jesse glanced up as the clouds floated away, revealing a star-filled sky. God had mercy on Oakton and spared them.

"It missed us." Emma straightened. Tears ran down her cheeks. "It wasn't like the last time."

He reached out to gather her back into his arms, but stopped as Tommy wrapped his arms around his father. "You're not dead," he said.

Jesse lifted his son. "No, I'm very much alive."

Ruth grabbed Emma to her. "I thought I'd lost you." She cupped Emma's face, wiping away her tears. "This is some spring, isn't it?" Without waiting for her granddaughter's reply, she turned to Jesse. "Would you be so kind as to ride out and check on Mr. Carson? With his leg still healing, he won't be able to run to shelter if caught unawares."

"I'll go as soon as Tommy is settled in bed."

"I'll care for him." Emma put a hand on his arm. "You go. There might be others who need you."

He nodded and brushed a loose strand of hair away from her face. "Thank you."

She took Tommy's hand and led him away, leaving Jesse to watch them go. He could have lost either one of them. That would have been the end of his world.

"You love her," Ruth said.

"I think so." It was hard to determine whether his feelings for her were those of a man grateful to a woman who cared about his son or whether he loved her as a man did toward a woman he wanted to marry. The feelings he felt for Emma were nothing to the ones he'd felt for Maureen.

Filled with confusion, he headed away to search for an automobile to borrow. It was times such as this that made him miss the one the storm had taken.

A farmer, in town stocking up on supplies, offered to give Jesse a ride out to the homes further out. As they drove, they noticed a few trees down, some broken branches, but none of the devastation from a few weeks ago. Jesse breathed a sigh of relief when they reached the Carson place and Mr. Carson waved to them from his front porch.

"It's nice of you to check up on me," he said. "But that storm completely passed me by. Missed the whole town, if I'm correct. It sure was a sight coming over the mountain."

"Ruth was worried about you." Jesse propped a foot on the bottom step. "It came as a surprise to Emma to hear about you two keeping company."

Mr. Carson grinned around a pipe stem in his mouth. "I reckon it did. Still, I'm not too old to get heart flutters when an attractive woman pays me attention."

Jesse laughed. "As long as your intentions are honorable, I've no complaints. See you next week when I take a look at that leg."

"Yep. You know, a doctor ought to have a car."

"I haven't needed one since the storm."

"I reckon if you had one now, Jones there would have been able to head on home." He waved at the man waiting in the truck.

"I suppose." What was he getting at?

"My brother passed away a month ago and left me his automobile. I heard yours was destroyed by the twister. I've already got a truck, so I don't need the car. I could give it to my sister, but her husband has enough money to feed all of Oakton for a month." He fished a set of keys from his pocket and tossed them to Jesse. "Merry Christmas, Happy Birthday, and my medical bill is paid in full."

"None of that comes close to the price of a car."

"I reckon that's for me to determine." Mr. Carson laughed. "Call it a loan, then."

"I'm much obliged. This will help me expand to the outlying areas." Jesse glanced over to where a black 1923 Biddle Sedan glowed under the stars. "She's a beauty."

"Wouldn't know. I prefer my Ford."

"Thank you." Jesse waved goodbye to Jones and slid behind the steering wheel of the Sedan. Tommy's eyes were going to bug from his head. Not to mention how he hoped Emma would feel.

"I'm taking Emma and the others for a picnic tomorrow," he called out the window. "We'll by out by your pond at noon. See you then!"

Unless Jesse was mistaken, Mr. Carson would leap at the chance to spend time with Ruth. Not to mention, it wouldn't hurt Emma to get to know the older man. It looked as if he planned on sticking around for a while.

Jesse caressed the steering wheel. Yep, he couldn't wait for Emma to see the new lady in his life.

13

After another stirring church service where the pastor again spoke on thankfulness, Emma set a canister of lemonade into a cardboard box. Once upon a time, Grandma had owned a lovely picnic basket. Now, they made do with whatever they could find. The lack of running water and electricity were the things she missed most. Although, she'd heard a rumor that morning that electricity should be restored within a day or two.

"Here are the sandwiches." Grandma handed her several wrapped in greased paper. "It's a perfect day for a picnic."

"Is it the picnic or where we're going that has you so lighthearted?" Emma smiled.

"Both." She glanced out the open door. "Jesse is in a good mood this morning. Almost like a child on Christmas."

"He's been that way since he got home last night." Emma placed a cake she'd baked that morning in the box with the other food and folded the lid closed. "We're ready."

"I've got the quilt." Tommy started to yank Grandma's wedding quilt from her cot.

"This one." Emma handed him a faded nine-block.

"Don't take the ones from the beds."

He raced away as the quilt unfolded and dragged behind him. Emma laughed. Was there anything more rambunctious than a six-year-old boy? She hefted the box of food and headed outside.

Jesse rushed forward and relieved her of the cumbersome box. "Your chariot awaits."

"It's beautiful." She ran her hand over the shiny black paint of the automobile. "Where in the world did you find it?"

"Mr. Carson gave it to me to pay off his medical bill." He grinned "A bit extravagant, but he said it was only sitting there."

"So this is why you've been so excited." She opened the door and climbed into the backseat, the front already occupied by Tommy. The leather squeaked under her as she settled into place. She clapped her hands for Annie to join them. "We'll be riding in style."

"Mr. Carson is a fine man," Grandma said, joining her.

Emma was beginning to believe so. He could have sold the car, rather than give it away. Instead, he'd chosen to help the community by making their doctor more mobile.

Soon, they bumped their way down the dirt road leading to Carson's ranch. The sun sat high overhead and a gentle breeze kept the temperature pleasant. Emma couldn't think of a better way to spend a Sunday afternoon than on a picnic with the people who mattered the most to her. Not to mention the fact that she now had the opportunity to get better acquainted with Grandma's beau.

Mr. Carson limped down his steps, leaning heavily

on a cane. "Welcome. I hope you don't mind that my nephew will be joining us later. My sister got the letter saying I'd been injured in the storm and sent Bill to check up on me."

"We don't mind at all, Mr. Carson," Emma said, exiting the automobile.

"Please, call me Jim."

"Very well." She took the refolded quilt from the back of the car and draped it over her arm. "Lead the way."

Tommy and Annie galloped ahead of them, leaping above budding wildflowers. They stopped at the edge of a lovely pond sparkling in the sun. A male mallard and his harem floated by, filling the air with their squawks.

Emma took a deep breath and closed her eyes, lifting her face to the sun. Nothing could possibly mar such a beautiful day. She opened one eye and checked the sky for clouds. Not a one. The day was perfect.

She stooped and spread out the quilt. Arranging the skirt of her dress around her knees, she sat and watched as Tommy and Jesse skipped rocks. Grandma and Jim strolled to the other side of the lake. Emma was alone.

Lying back, she stared at the bluebonnet sky. Perhaps she could squeeze in a nap before the others returned for lunch. She smiled, envisioning the wickedness of wasting the day away sleeping. Or, she could read the romance novel she'd stuck in the picnic box. Either way, she planned on doing absolutely nothing for the rest of the day. She flung her arms wide and fell back.

A shadow fell across her face. "Sleeping beauty. Perhaps I should awaken her with true love's kiss."

Her eyes shot open. Staring down at her was the last person she ever wanted to see again. Bill Hudson, her almost ex-fiance.

The day was ruined.

She bolted to her feet. "What are you doing here?"

"Attending a picnic." His green eyes sparkled. Once, she'd thought him handsome. Now that she knew the heart that beat inside his chest, she found him repulsive. "I wondered where you had run off to."

"I see you've met my nephew," Jim said, joining them.

Emma straightened her arm and pointed. "This is your nephew!"

Jim nodded, his smile fading. "Do the two of you know each other?"

Bill laid his arm across Emma's shoulders. "Of course, we do. After all, I proposed to her six months ago."

~

Jesse's steps faltered. Emma was engaged?

"And I said no." She moved away from him. "I made myself more than clear when you asked."

He shrugged. "Just wedding jitters."

"You're delusional." Emma marched to Jesse's side. "Save me," she whispered.

"Play along." Jesse pulled her close, planting a kiss on the tip of her nose. "I don't see how she can marry you, Mr. Hudson, when she's engaged to me."

Tommy's eyes widened. He opened his mouth to speak and snapped it shut when Jesse shook his head. He would have a lot of explaining to do to his son later. Now, if they could only get through the day until the man left.

Bill's eyes narrowed. "It seems Emma moves quickly."

"I don't know about that," Jesse said. "But, now that you know, it's best if you leave."

The other man laughed. "I'm here for the next few months. My dear father wants me to learn the cattle business. It seems as if we'll both be vying for Emma's affections."

Not to mention that Jesse also feared Jonah Spencer had his eye on her. The situation surrounding the lovely Miss Larson was quickly becoming ridiculous enough to rival a movie picture he'd seen last year. In the show, *A Covered Wagon*, men had vied for the attention of a lovely lady who wanted to ride a horse. Jesse felt like one of those men.

He thrust out his hand. "May the best man win."

"For heaven's sake." Emma stomped her foot. "Both of you stop strutting around like roosters and let's get this picnic over with. This is the very reason a man does not figure into my future." She plopped onto the quilt and tossed sandwiches toward everyone like cards being dealt in a game of poker.

Luckily, Ruth poured the lemonade or Jesse feared they'd all be wearing the drink instead of holding it in a glass. She met his gaze and shrugged. Clearly, she knew very little of her granddaughter's life before Oakton. "Let's take a walk, Jim, and let these young people work out their problems."

Jim nodded, grabbed his sandwich and lemonade, and limped after Ruth.

"So, you aren't engaged to this man?" Bill asked.

"What?" She glanced up, then at Jesse. "Oh, yes, of course, I am. You've got me flustered is all."

"When is the wedding?"

"At the end of summer," Jesse said, biting into his ham and cheese sandwich. "Before school starts again."

"You're going to let your wife pursue a career?" His eyes widened as if the thought was ludicrous.

"Why not? Why should a woman give up her dream because she gets married?" Jesse tossed Emma a grin.

She rolled her eyes and looked away.

Why was she mad at him? He was only trying to help her get rid of someone she clearly wanted nothing to do with. She asked him for help, not the other way around. The least she could do was show some gratitude.

"A woman needs to be at home, keeping house, taking care of the children, and making a good impression on her husband's business associates."

Jesse's sandwich got stuck in his throat. If looks could kill, Emma's gaze would have slaughtered the foolish man. "I agree, to an extent, but in today's age, not all women are content to be just a mother and a wife."

"Maybe if men put their feet down, we wouldn't even be having this discussion."

"I'm glad the two of you have this all worked out." Emma stood and tossed the wrapper to her sandwich in the box. "As an independent woman who has had a perfectly good afternoon spoiled, I am taking a walk around the pond ...alone." She marched away, her ponytail bobbing around her shoulders.

Bill shook his head. "I'll never be able to figure out women."

"Isn't that the truth?" Jesse watched her go,

wanting nothing more than to follow. But, having been married before, he knew that when a woman said she wanted to be alone, it was best to let her be.

He started cleaning up the picnic supplies, then shooed Bill off the quilt so he could fold it. Once he had everything stashed back into his car, he crossed his arms and waited for the others to return.

Emma was right. The day was ruined. Still, the competition with Bill, which might have started off as a ploy to get the man to go away, might be an interesting turn of events. Pretending to be Emma's fiancé stirred his heart. He found he liked the idea, and now wanted the other man to stick around for a while so Jesse cold keep pretending that Emma belonged to him.

Over time, their masquerade might turn into something real, and Tommy would have a new mother.

Bill thrust out his hand. "May the best man win."

"Yep." Jesse returned the shake a bit harder than he normally would. "Nothing is final until the vows have been said."

"I am not a prize heifer to be auctioned off." Emma glared from a few feet away. "I've a mind to send both of you packing."

Jesse leaned against the car. "Kind of hard to do when we live under the same roof."

"You live with him?" Bill's voice rose. "I could barely steal a kiss, but you're living in sin with him?"

"Hush." Emma squeezed past them and into the car. "You'll scare the cows with your screeching. It isn't what you think. Not that it's any of your business, but Grandma lives with us, as does Jesse's son. It's a temporary arrangement until suitable housing can be built. It is all quite proper."

"What about your reputation?"

"Once the town finds out that I'm engaged, nothing will be as it was." She slammed the door.

Jesse sighed. She was right. Once the gossip mongers got wind of the engagement, false or otherwise, and discovered there was another man in the picture, nothing would be peaceful again.

14

"Would you mind telling me what happened this afternoon?" Grandma rolled over on the bed to face Emma.

The question was bound to come sooner or later. Especially after the ridiculous farce Jesse had gotten her into. No, not him. Emma did it to herself with her whispered plea for help.

"Bill Hudson proposed to me in St. Louis." She twisted the thin sheet in her hand over them. "When I caught him stepping out with a fellow teacher at the school I taught at, I broke it off with him. It turns out, she wasn't the only lady he'd been spending time with other than me. Now that he's seen me again, he wants to resume where we left off." Something she didn't have the slightest desire to do.

"And Jesse?"

"I asked him for help. I had no idea he was going to pretend that we were getting married." A tear trailed down her cheek. "I've made such a mess of things."

Grandma patted her hand. "Nothing that can't be undone. My suggestion is to let things ride and see what happens. Maybe you'll come to realize that being engaged to Jesse isn't a bad thing."

"I haven't planned on marriage for a very long time. Men haven't been the most reliable people where I'm concerned."

"Then, you just haven't met the right ones." She kissed Emma's cheek. "Goodnight, sweetheart. Don't fret. It will all be fine." She turned her back. Within seconds, gentle snores replaced her whispers.

Sleep didn't come as easily to Emma. Instead, her mind jumped from one thought to another, like the clips of a movie show she'd seen once. She gasped and bolted upright. She needed to talk to Jesse right away.

Grabbing her robe, she slipped from the bed and padded into the room he shared with Tommy. "Jesse?"

"What's wrong?" He seemed instantly awake.

"I need to speak with you."

"Now?" He ran his hands through his hair, causing the strands to stick up on end.

While she couldn't see much more than shadows without lighting a lantern, she could imagine how much he looked like Tommy at that moment. "It's important."

He shuffled to their dining area and slouched in a kitchen chair. "You aren't ill? Ruth is fine?"

"Yes." She sat across from him, doing her best not to notice how the moonlight through the window Jesse had someone cut the other day highlighted his muscular chest. She failed. He was a fine looking man and no doubt about it. "It's about the charade you came up with."

He frowned. "You want to talk about this now?"

"I won't be able to sleep otherwise." She wanted to light a lantern so he could see how important this was, but providing light would only emphasize the fact she was in her nightgown, and he slept in nothing more than a pair of cotton pants. If anyone found out …

"My teaching contract clearly states that I am not to be married while under contract."

He nodded. "I thought of that, which is why I said we would marry in the summer."

"I'm also not supposed to enter into a romantic relationship with the parent of one of my students."

He scrubbed his hands down his face. "I see your dilemma, but it's too late to think clearly. Do you really think Bill will go around town shouting the news? I rather figured he would welcome the competition between him and I. You're probably worked up over nothing."

Competition? "I'm a prize to be won in a contest?" The conversation was only reinforcing her reasons for not wanting to get married. Maybe Grandma was right, and there were good men in the world, but she wasn't meant to find one. She slumped in her seat.

Who was she kidding? Jesse Baxter was one of the good guys. No matter how much she tried to put the blame on him, she had no one to blame but herself. It was time to be accountable for her own actions. She should have stood her ground with Bill and not involved a third party.

"He doesn't strike me as the type to stick around for long. If we can keep up the pretense for a few weeks, he'll transfer his attention elsewhere."

"I hope you're right. The man can be exhausting."

He planted his hands on the table and pushed to his feet. "I'm sorry if I caused you more problems, but you did ask for my help. That's the best I could come up with on the spur of the moment. Is the thought of being engaged to me so repulsive?"

"What? No!" She stood. "It's only ... I've worked hard to get my teaching certificate. I don't want to be terminated over a misunderstanding."

"We'll make sure that doesn't happen. If it comes down to that, we call off the engagement, showing anyone who cares that you chose your career over your fiancé. Goodnight."

He shuffled back to bed, leaving Emma feeling as if she had actually wounded the man she intended to marry.

Why did life have to be complicated? Ever since she was a child, she'd had her future planned. College, career, marriage to a man as wonderful as her father, children. In that order. The death of her parents started the spin that spun her future on its axis. She had thought accepting the teaching job in Oakton and caring for Grandma would have put things back into a pattern.

She sighed and headed back to bed. Lying there, staring through the dark at the ceiling, she asked God what she was doing wrong. He didn't answer. Finally, her mind slowed, her eyes grew heavy, and she slept.

~

Despite the late night conversation with Emma, Jesse woke refreshed and ready to face the day. He still thought her fears unreasonable. It was 1925, after all. Ten years ago, the rules for teachers were much more strict. The people of Oakton wouldn't care one way or the other whether their teacher was in a relationship or not. Especially not one with their local doctor.

He planted a kiss on Tommy's head, grabbed a cup of coffee and headed to the clinic. With search and rescue completed, he spent most of his day reading the newspaper. Not that he was complaining. The lack of illness and injury was a good thing.

As he unlocked the clinic door, he spotted Bill and Marilyn deep in conversation. From their grins and body language, flirtation was in full swing. Jesse smiled. It didn't take the man long to give up on Emma.

He shoved the door open, flipped on the light, grateful that the clinic was one of the first places where electricity was restored in town, and set his mug on his desk. He bent to retrieve the newspapers he had delivered each morning, despite the fact the news was a couple of days old by the time he received them.

"Good morning." Bill entered the clinic, one hand pressed to his stomach.

"Have you come to tell me you're going to leave Emma alone?"

"Why would I do that?" Bill sat in a chair reserved for patients, propped his feet on Jesse's desk, and crossed his ankles. "No, I have a medical problem."

Jesse refrained from saying anything in regards to the man's moral health and took his seat behind his desk. "What are your symptoms?"

"I've had this sharp pain in my side since late yesterday afternoon. I thought at first it was something I'd eaten, but it's getting worse."

Not bad enough to keep the man from chasing skirts. "Let's head into my examining room so you can lie down." Jesse led him to the partitioned off portion of the railroad car.

Bill climbed on the table and lay down.

"Any nausea or vomiting?" Jesse shook the thermometer. Now that he took a closer look at the man, his skin was pale except for high spots of color in each cheek.

"I vomited this morning. I haven't had much of an appetite since yesterday."

"Hold this under your tongue for me." He slid the thermometer under Bill's tongue before taking the man's pulse. "Slightly elevated." He removed the thermometer. "Your temperature is 102. Show me where it hurts."

"Right here." Bill pointed to a spot a few inches down and to the right of his belly button. His stomach looked slightly bloated.

Jesse pressed on the spot. Bill groaned when he released the pressure.

"I think your appendix is inflamed. I'm going to have you transported to the hospital in Harrisburg." He reached for the newly installed phone. He could have been running the clinic in a brand new building, but the railroad car worked fine for now. He'd decided last week to let other businesses go first.

"I can drive myself." Bill struggled to a sitting position. "Or you can drive me in my car."

"Then, how will I get back?"

"I don't know. All I know is that I'm dying."

"You aren't dying."

"I will if I don't get this cut out of me." Bill staggered to the door. "Tell Emma that she can have you. I've got to get back to the city where medical attention isn't an hour away."

Jesse sighed and grabbed his hat. He couldn't let the man drive in his condition. "Wait for me." He turned the sign on his door to closed. With a glance at the library, he climbed behind the wheel of Bill's Ford. Jesse would have to take a cab home.

"I've got to stop and let my son know I'm

leaving."

Bill waved a hand. "Hurry."

Jesse stopped in front of the library and dashed inside. He explained the circumstances to Emma and Tommy. "I'm sorry, but if I don't drive him, he might collapse on the side of the road somewhere."

"I understand," Emma said. "Bill has never been one to listen to reason."

Jesse gave a nod and raced back to the car. "All ready to go."

"Looks like you win after all," Bill said, leaning his head against the back of the seat and closing his eyes.

"Not much of a competition, was it?" He almost told the man it had all been a ruse, but Bill might feel differently about letting Emma go once he recovered from his surgery.

"I don't know what I was thinking. She's too good for me. That's the kind of woman a man settles down with." He opened one eye and peered at Jesse. "Am I right?"

"Completely." Maybe he wouldn't say anything to anyone about his silly little plan. What was the harm in waiting to see how things turned out between them? He wanted to ask Bill if he had told anyone about Jesse and Emma. Did it matter?

"How soon after she got here did you and Emma become an item?"

"Right after the twister."

Bill chuckled, then clutched his stomach. "You move faster than I do. Did you ever think that a killer storm could blow a woman like her into your arms?"

"No, I never did."

Bill fell asleep, leaving Jesse to make the rest of the drive in silence. It took an hour to get the man situated into a hospital bed and scheduled for surgery. While Jesse could have performed the operation, he wanted to get home. If he hurried, he'd be there by supper time.

He rented a cab and spent the drive back deep in thought as to how he could convince Emma to let him court her without the shadow of pretense. Considering their talk the night before, and her admitting how much her career meant to her, he doubted she would be open to it.

But, his son needed a mother. Jesse was quickly growing to care very much for Emma, and couldn't think of anyone he'd rather marry. It was settled. He'd figure out how to accomplish his goal when he got home.

Once home, he paid the cab driver an astronomical amount, which he fully intended to send a bill to Bill Hudson for. He turned and came face-to-face with Ruth.

"Jesse," she said. "I have a brilliant plan to get my Emma married, if you're willing to help me."

15

The coy glances Grandma cast Emma's way at breakfast set her nerves on edge. What was the dear woman up to now? Rather than spend too much time dwelling on Grandma's strange behavior, Emma ate her eggs at record speed and headed to school. She'd watch for Tommy from the library door. After yesterday's fiasco at the picnic, she couldn't face Jesse early in the day.

"Good morning, Miss Larson." Fred Harper stopped sweeping the sidewalk in front of his store. "I hear there's good news on the horizon."

"Oh?" She scanned the surrounding area. "Is your building next in line to be rebuilt? That is wonderful news."

He laughed and resumed sweeping. "Keep your secrets, if you must, but word is spreading."

He must mean the upcoming recital. Emma smiled and increased her pace. Of course the town would be excited. After the twister's devastation and the weeks of hard work rebuilding their town, the recital provided the town with a welcome respite.

"Good morning, Miss Larson." Mae Jennings strolled by, a wicker basket swinging from one arm.

"Good morning. You're out and about early." Emma dug in her pocketbook for the keys to the library.

"Hungry boarders. I hear tell they're building the school building next week," Mae said. "But I reckon it might be empty come summer." She winked.

"Well, of course it will be." Emma jammed the key into the lock. "There's no school in the summer." Oh, when she got her hands on Bill, she'd throttle him! The man must have wasted no time in letting everyone within hearing distance know that Emma had a secret romance going on with Jesse. Not so secret, or true.

It was good news that in a short time she wouldn't have to hold school in a corner of the library. She missed her large chalkboard and bookshelf. The flag that stood proudly in one corner. She even missed the wood burning stove that had a tendency to smoke.

She glanced to the church down the street. Almost rebuilt. She sent a prayer of thanksgiving heavenward to know the town valued education enough to schedule the rebuilding of the school next. With donations still arriving from neighboring towns and cities, Oakton would be back to its former beauty in no time.

"I'm here!" Tommy pushed past her, depositing his lunch pail under the table he used as a desk. "What do you want me to do first?"

"The primary spelling words need copied, the chairs need to be set out, and the slates placed in each spot with pieces of chalk." Emma hung her purse on a hook. "Which would you like to do?"

He planted his small fists on his hips, scrunched up his face, and surveyed the room. "I reckon I can set out the slates."

Emma turned to hide her smile. "They're stacked

on the table over there." While he did that, she collected the chairs scattered around the library and pushed them against the tables.

"Aren't you the sly one." The librarian, Miss Dillow, leaned against a table, her wrinkled face creased with a grin. "I never would have thought you the type to give up teaching after only one year because of a handsome man."

Emma bit her tongue to keep from telling the truth. She couldn't help but wonder which would be worse; telling the truth and letting everyone in town know about her private business regarding Bill, or to keep the secret alive by not saying anything? Either way, someone was going to get hurt. If she didn't marry Jesse, she'd be labeled a heart breaker. If she did marry him, she might feel as if she had no choice and come to resent him.

What a conundrum. "You never really can tell about someone, can you?" Emma grimaced as she continued the lie. There had to be a way out of this.

Miss Dillow chuckled. "Especially the sweet, quiet ones." She headed to her desk, leaving Emma to drown in her deceit.

It took every ounce of strength she had to get through the school day. She went through the motions of teaching reading, writing, and arithmetic, even managing to carve time out of the afternoon for recital plans and rehearsal. By the time the day ended, she sent Tommy home without her and collapsed at her desk.

Maybe Grandma would be willing to move somewhere no one knew them. They could get lost in St. Louis, or head south to Little Rock. Silly woman. She sighed. Grandma grew up in Oakton. She wouldn't leave short of death.

Emma stood and grabbed her purse, saying goodbye to Miss Dillow. Jesse was right. She should probably let things proceed. Either she would welcome marriage to a wonderful man who she was quickly growing to love, or she could embrace spinsterhood as the librarian had. Either way, her future was in God's hands. Who was she to fight against something already set into motion? She certainly was a wishy-washy woman who didn't know her heart or her mind.

She stepped outside to the sight of Jesse crossing the street to meet his son. He put a hand on Tommy's shoulder, whispered something in his ear, and glanced Emma's way. He waved. "We're heading to the store for a grape soda. Would you like to join us?"

Tears sprang to her eyes. He was a good man. One who always put others first. Grandma was right. Emma could do a lot worse than pretend to be engaged to Jesse Baxter. She smiled through her tears. "I'd love to."

~

Jesse almost mentioned Emma's tear-filled eyes, then decided against it. Maureen had had her moments of emotion; moments when commenting on them often resulted in a verbal lashing tossed his way.

Instead, he kept Tommy between them and talked about nothing in particular during the short walk to the store. He smiled down at her as he opened the door and let her enter first.

"There's the happy couple." Fred beamed. "What can I get for you?"

"Three grape sodas," Jesse said, avoiding looking at Emma.

"Got some cold ones." He dug in a red metal

cooler and handed three bottles to Jesse.

Jesse handed them to Tommy so he could open them using the opener on the side of the cooler. Few things pleased his son more than opening soda bottles.

Cold drinks in hand, they headed back outside. "We've time enough before supper to sit by the lake," Jesse said. "Once summer hits, the afternoons won't be as pleasant."

Emma nodded, then lifted her drink to her lips. Her throat moved as she swallowed.

"Dad looks at you, Miss Larson, just like he looked at Mom before she died."

Emma choked, then spewed soda over the front of Jesse's white shirt. Her eyes widened and she gasped for breath.

Jesse pounded on her back. "What in the world possessed you to say such a thing, son?"

"It's true. You look at my teacher like you love her." Clutching his bottle by the neck, he raced toward the lake.

"Are you all right?" Jesse studied Emma's red face. "Can you speak?"

"I'm ... fine." She wasn't choking, she was laughing.

Jesse scratched his head. Had he missed something? What could she possibly find humorous in her being compared to his dead wife? "I apologize for Tommy. He doesn't think before speaking."

"I'm sorry," she wheezed. "He does have a knack for saying the unexpected."

"I won't argue with that." He crooked his arm for her to take.

She slipped her hand through the curve of his

elbow and wiped her streaming eyes on the sleeve of her blouse. "Gracious, that boy makes me laugh."

"I seem to recall another time when you stated that the Baxter men made you laugh."

Her face reddened, not from laughing this time. "You're horrible for reminding me. I could have permanently injured you." The corner of her mouth twitched.

"You may laugh. But, I assure you, I will keep my distance in further water adventures."

A giggle, as delightful as a bird's trill, escaped her. "Stop. You're making it very difficult for me to enjoy the pleasure of this soda." She sat on a bench provided for seating.

The sun cast sparkles as brilliant as diamonds across the water and in her eyes. Jesse sat beside her, placing an arm along the back of the bench. A couple of inches more and his arm would rest on her shoulders. Would she welcome his touch or be offended?

His gaze flicked to her lips, stained purple by the soda. What if he kissed her? Tasted the soda through her lips?

"Look, Dad!"

Tommy held up what was left of a fish skeleton, effectively erasing any romantic thoughts Jesse might have. "How do you think it died?"

"I need to figure out a way of ridding him of this obsession."

"He'll figure it out in time." Emma shaded her eyes with one hand. "Losing his mother the way he did, watching her grow sicker with each passing day, is bound to have a long-lasting effect on someone so young."

Not to mention the way it effected a husband riddled with guilt. Jesse stood. "Put that down, son, and come wash your hands." It's a miracle he hasn't contacted some kind of fatal disease.

Taking a hold of Tommy's arm, Jesse marched back to their tin can of a home and ignored the questioning look in Emma's eyes as to his abrupt change of mood. He plunged Tommy's hands into the warm sudsy water set aside for dishes, scrubbed them, then ordered his son to prepare fresh water for the dishes. Once he had significantly proven to everyone around him that he was a total cad, he stormed to his bed, threw himself on it, and covered his eyes with his arm. He would apologize for acting like a child later.

It was his fault Tommy was obsessed with dead things. It was his fault Maureen had died frightened and alone. He'd cut his doctoring in half in order to be at her side during her final days, but an accident had pulled him away. Instead of letting someone else handle the emergency, he'd rushed off, grateful to escape the sadness of her dying, if only for a few minutes.

When he'd returned home, exhausted and disheartened at the loss of his patient, Maureen had been dead. Lost in grief and guilt, Jesse had only recently established a relatively normal routine for his son. Still, despite his efforts to be a good father, Tommy was obsessed with anything dead. He desperately needed a mother.

"Are you finished sulking?"

He opened his eyes to see Ruth in the doorway.

"Because your supper is getting cold, not to mention that this type of behavior won't help our plan any."

"I know that." He swung his legs over the side of the bed. Couldn't a man wallow in self-pity for five minutes? "I'll just flat out ask."

"That won't work. If I know my granddaughter as well as I think I do, she'll be hurt and angry. This has to be done correctly. Now, come eat the soup I've prepared."

How could Emma ever think her grandmother suffered from dementia? The woman was one of the sharpest people Jesse had ever met.

He sighed and stood. He might as well paste on a smile and continue with the plan.

16

"**That Tennessee schoolteacher**, John T. Scopes, was arrested for teaching the theory of evolution." Jesse said, rattling his morning newspaper.

"He should have known better." Emma dropped a ladle. "It's against the law to teach about evolution in the public school system." It amazed her that some people actually believed humans came from fish who sprouted legs, but Americans had the freedom to think what they would. For the most part, anyway. "What else does your paper say?"

"Hitler wrote a book." Jesse closed the paper. "I'd like to read good news once in a while."

"I have good news," Ruth said. "The insurance check on my house came in yesterday. We can start rebuilding and get out of this tin can."

"Tommy and I won't be here much—"

Someone banged on the door. Emma's hand shook as she poured coffee into Jesse's mug. Some of the liquid splashed, burning her hand. She hissed and headed for the cooler water in a porcelain jug.

"Let me take a look at that." Jesse reached for her, but stopped when the person knocking on the door cried for help. He yanked open the door.

A man Emma didn't know stood on the steps, cradling a young child in his arms. "She's burning up, Doc. We need you."

"Go. I'll see to Tommy." Emma dipped a rag in the cool water and soothed the ache on her hand.

"Thank you." Jesse grabbed his black medical bag from the table and rushed after the man, both running to the clinic next door.

"This happened before." Tommy threw his spoon across the room and dashed out the door.

Emma met Grandma's startled gaze. "I'll go after him." She dropped the rag into the water and hurried outside. Tommy was already across the street and headed for the woods. Unless she found him quickly, she'd never be able to start school on time.

"Go." Grandma placed a hand on her shoulder. "Your worry is written on your face. I'll open the school and occupy the students all day if I have to."

"God bless you. The day's lesson plans are in my bag." Emma sprinted after the runaway.

This early in the morning, the woods were dark and ominous. Much too frightening for a young boy to wander around in alone. "Tommy?" She slapped a low-hanging branch away from her face and headed to the only spot she was familiar with—the creek.

She found Tommy furiously throwing rocks into the water. When he struggled with one too heavy for him to lift on his own, she rushed forward to help. They hefted the rock into the water with a loud plop.

"I need more," Tommy said, scanning the ground.

"Then, we'll find more." Emma kicked off her shoes and waded into the creek. The hem of her dress soaked with cool water and floated around her knees.

She tossed whatever rocks she could find on the bank for Tommy to throw back in. As long as he had the energy to toss, she'd keep giving him ammunition.

A few minutes later, he crumpled to the ground and sobbed.

Emma sloshed from the water and knelt beside him, pulling him into her arms. "Are you ready to tell me what's got you in such a state?"

"Somebody is going to die." His cries increased and he buried his face in her chest.

"Why do you say that?" She rubbed her hand in small circles on his back.

"The last time someone interrupted Dad at a meal, Mom died."

Tears sprang to Emma's eyes and clogged her throat. "Oh, sweetie, I don't think that's going to happen this time. Your father is a doctor. People are going to need him."

He sniffed. "Something bad will happen. You'll see."

A crashing in the brush had Emma scrambling to her knees. She thrust Tommy behind her as Annie bounded toward them.

"I see your friend has come to offer comfort." She smiled as the puppy jumped on Tommy with abandon.

Emma perched on a fallen log and watched them play. How could she convince the poor child that not everyone took sick and died because his father didn't get to finish breakfast? How horrible to go through life at such a young age, waiting for disaster to strike again.

She slid to the ground, using the log as a backrest and stretched out her legs. Other than trying to be a constant in Tommy's life and provide him with a sense of structure and safety, she couldn't do much else. He needed a mother. But, it might be too soon for him and his father to entertain such a thought.

She plucked at some nearby grass. How would she feel if Jesse were to marry and another woman took Emma's place in Tommy's heart, relegating her to only the child's teacher rather than a close family friend? As if she'd lost something precious, that's how. She swiped the back of her hand across her face and removed the tears that had escaped.

If only a dog's kisses could cheer her as easily as it had Tommy. She should get up and head to the school, but lazing in the morning sun next to a babbling creek with a giggling boy and barking dog seemed like a much better way to spend the time. She spread the bottom of her dress out to dry and leaned her head back.

"Tommy? Look at the clouds. What do you see?"

He plopped down next to her. "A pirate ship."

She could see it, maybe, if she squinted, how the large cloud could look like a ship in full sail. "What else?"

"An angel! It turned into an angel. Like magic." His eyes widened and focused on her. "Did you see it?"

"I did." She smiled. The clouds parted and thinned to loosely resemble an angel with wings, but she'd agree to almost anything to keep a smile on his face and the tears from his eyes.

Tommy crossed his arms behind his head and leaned back. "Sometimes, God sends us a gift just when we need it the most."

Her smile widened. "Yes, He does.

~

By lunchtime, Jesse wanted the day to be over. His

first patient at breakfast had been the first of many. Influenza seemed to have struck Oakton a bit late that year, and made its presence known with a vengeance.

He washed his hands for the hundredth time that day and glanced out the door to see Emma and Tommy exiting the forest and heading for the school. Just as he'd decided to close for lunch and see why neither of them was in school yet, a frantic mother bustled toward him. Just when he'd given up on eating at all in the near future, Ruth entered the clinic, a basket on her arm.

"I am here to help," she said. She set the basket on his desk, patted a little girl with fever-reddened cheeks on the head, and bustled to the back room, only to return with a basin of water and a rag. "Lay this across the back of your little one's neck," she told the mother. "Dr. Baxter will be with you as soon as he can."

"Thank you." Gratitude for her help overwhelmed Jesse.

"I would have been here sooner," she said, washing a thermometer, "but I had to cover at the school while Emma fetched Tommy."

"Why?" His head jerked up.

"After you were pulled away from breakfast, he shot out the door like a cannon ball." She carefully placed the clean instrument on a towel. "Said something about it having happened before." She turned with a smile and hurried to greet an elderly woman arriving. In her hands, the patient carried a bowl.

"Let me rinse that out for you." Ruth took the bowl, ushered the woman into a waiting chair, and then set the bowl onto the washboard. "Gracious, Jesse, you're going to be here all day. There isn't a lot you can do for influenza, you know."

"I'm aware of that." He smiled at the child in front of him, handed the mother the directions for making a poultice that would help with chest congestion, and turned to the next patient. "We can help make them more comfortable. Tell me more about my son."

Jesse thought back to the morning Maureen had died. He'd been called away that morning at breakfast, too. No wonder Tommy took off. Jesse glanced at the next two waiting patients. If he were lucky, the rush would be over soon, and he could reassure his son that things were fine. That they would remain fine.

All his life Jesse had wanted to be a doctor. For the first time, he wondered about his choice of career. If Maureen were still alive, he wouldn't have to worry about how his job affected his son. But now ... he shook his head. Death was an all too common occurrence. Something Tommy was too young to understand, and Jesse was too busy to explain.

"When this influenza runs its course," Ruth said, "you should take Tommy somewhere fun. Spend some time with the boy away from the daily life you two have."

"That is an excellent idea." It would do them both good to get away for a few days. A telegram to St. Louis would insure the town had a substitute doctor. "We'll leave this weekend."

He'd take Tommy camping, something Jesse's father used to do for him. He spent the rest of the afternoon caring for patients with upset stomachs, fevers, and congestion, while his mind focused on the pleasure of spending lazy afternoons fishing.

The sounds of children racing down the sidewalk

alerted him to the fact school was out for the day. "I don't want Tommy in here, Ruth. Please make sure he stays away. I don't need for him to be sick."

"If he's going to be sick, he'll be sick." She thrust her hands into a bucket of disinfecting water. "But, I'll keep him away. Make sure you eat something."

He nodded so she would know he had heard her and moved to the next patient. By the time he finished, the sun hung low in the sky, his back ached, and his head pounded. He chalked the symptoms off to exhaustion and locked the clinic.

"Hey, Dad." Tommy glanced up from the table where he worked on homework.

"Evening, son." Jesse patted him on the head and passed through to his bed. "I'll see you in the morning."

"But, you just got home." Tommy dashed after him.

"Don't come any closer." Jesse held up a finger. "I don't know whether I'm sick or tired, but I don't want to risk it."

Emma stood behind Tommy. "You go ahead and hug your father if you want." She lifted her chin as if daring him to argue.

Tommy gave him a quick hug and went back to the table.

"What are you doing?" Jesse plopped on the side of his bed.

"Easing a little boy's fears. Influenza or not, you're all he has. I spent the morning doing my best to take his mind off the fact that someone else in his life is going to die. You came home and reinforced those fears."

"I didn't know." His shoulders sagged. "Have him come read to me while I go to sleep."

Her face softened. "Have you eaten?"

"A little from the basket your grandmother brought."

"I'll have Tommy bring you some soup."

He nodded and laid back, listening as she explained to his son how working all day making people feel better had left him tired. Emma was doing what Jesse should have been doing. Tired or not, he was the parent. It was his responsibility to make sure his child's needs were met.

He took a deep breath and sat up. "I'm coming to the table."

Tommy grinned and set a bowl in front of Jesse. "Miss Larson told me you're only tired. I'm not worried. I saw an angel in the sky today."

Jesse glanced up and met Emma's gaze. "Thank you."

He didn't need to look at the clouds. There was an angel standing right in front of him.

17

The heated look Jesse had given Emma at supper warmed her through the night, and she didn't think it because he had developed a fever or taken ill. The man was quickly falling for her and she had no idea how she felt about it. Sometimes her heart leaped for joy. At other times, it sank in despair.

She sat on the edge of her cot and buried her face in her hands. Why couldn't she make up her mind? Jesse wasn't Bill or Jonah. Why couldn't she let herself trust him?

With the recital in less than two week's time, she couldn't dwell on her vacillating feelings. She slipped her feet into her shoes and grabbed her teaching bag. School must go on.

Jesse sat alone at the table. When she entered, he slammed the newspaper closed.

"You look rested," she said.

"Very. I'm not ill, as I suspected. Just tired." His smile looked forced.

"What's wrong?" She glanced at an envelope on the table. The return address was from the school board. She fixed her gaze back on Jesse. "What did you read in the paper?"

"They aren't going to rebuild the school. With so

many people moving instead of rebuilding, they said we no longer have the student numbers to warrant the funds. School will end in Oakton and the students bussed to Harrisburg for the next school year. I'm sorry."

She sagged against the table. What was she going to do? She'd be unemployed in two weeks. She and Grandma had no choice now. They'd have to move. She stiffened. No, Emma would have to move, alone. Grandma would marry Mr. Carson. She hooked her purse over her arm, shoved the envelope into the pocket of her dress, and dashed outside.

She ducked around the corner and bent over, balancing her hands on her knees. Her breath came in gasps. The world grew fuzzy.

"Breath slowly." Jesse put an arm around her shoulders. "Things will be fine."

"How can you say that?" She jerked upright. "You have a job. You have a home being built." Her and Grandma did, too, but they'd have to sell. "I'm being left with nothing." Tears burned her eyes. She blinked them back. She would not cry. She'd shed enough tears since the disastrous twister.

"You could work for me." He put his hands on her shoulders. "Although it hasn't been said, we both know Ruth will marry Mr. Carson. She won't be able to help me in the clinic, and I can always use a level-headed assistant."

She jerked free. "I'm a teacher!" She stomped away and headed for the library.

"Hello, doll." Jonah leaned against the red brick wall.

"Go away." She inserted her key in the door. "I've

got to get ready for school."

"Why do you keep pushing me away?" He held the door closed. "You're the prettiest thing this town has to offer, and until I can convince these hillbillies to sell the land they hold so tight-fisted, we could have a good time."

"I'm a school teacher. I don't believe in good times." Just ask her grandmother or Jesse.

"I could show you how to have fun."

"I'm not interested." She shoved him aside. "Have a good day."

Inside, she leaned against the door and blinked back more tears. She was simply overwhelmed with the changes in her life. That was all. She wasn't normally such a cry baby.

She squared her shoulders and marched to her desk. She would make the most of the next two weeks and come up with another plan for her future. There was nothing that could be done at that moment to change anything. All she could do was make the best of what she had at that moment.

Thirty minutes later, she rang the bell and watched, with no small measure of sadness, as the students raced to the building. She had ten days to make an impact on their young lives. Then, they'd be handed off to someone else. She shook off her melancholy mood and forced a smile to her face, praying none of the parents had informed their children of the recent news from the paper.

At lunch, she opened the envelope from the school board. She scanned the contents. She wasn't out of a job, only relocate, if she wanted. She stared out the window to where the students played. She could still be some of these children's teacher. Then, her gaze fell on Tommy and confusion clouded her mind again. Was she content to only be his teacher? What about Jesse? Did she want to stay in Oakton and see if anything came of their masquerade engagement? The job opportunity in Harrisburg gave her the out she needed.

She read the letter again, and sighed. She had to give the board her answer by the end of the school year. How could she untangle the feelings in her heart in such a short time?

Approaching footsteps pulled her from her thoughts. She turned to see Grandma approaching with a basket.

"You ran off this morning without your lunch." She smiled and set the basket on the desk.

"I'm not very hungry, but thank you."

Grandma sat at the nearest table used for a desk and folded her hands on the surface. "Jesse told me of the school closing. Have you decided what you're going to do?"

She shrugged. "They offered me a teaching position in Harrisburg."

"Are you going to take it?"

"I don't know what to do."

"Mr. Carson asked me to marry him." Grandma smiled. "Not until the end of summer, though. If your decision hinges on leaving me alone, then that is no longer a concern." Her smile faded. "But, I hate you going away and being alone. I think maybe we should get you married."

"For heaven's sake, Grandma. Marriage is not always the answer." Emma shook her head. "I have two weeks to make my decision. Let me make it on my own."

She rose to ring the bell, signaling the end of recess. After a quick head count as the students filed inside, she realized Tommy was once again missing.

~

Not if Jesse had anything to do with it. He stepped behind a bookshelf to keep from being seen.

Ruth wasn't the only one who had noticed Emma left without her lunch. He sighed and stared at the bag in his hand. It looked as if he'd be eating two sandwiches from the diner.

He skirted around the edge of the library and out the back. So, Emma didn't want anyone interfering with her decision. He grinned. He would see about that.

Once he filled Ruth and Tommy in on his plan, their camping group of two would grow to four. Emma wouldn't be able to deny her attraction for him surrounded by nature with none of the distractions of the town or her students.

He went back to the clinic, grateful not to see anymore influenza victims. After yesterday, he needed a slow day of waiting on minor injuries.

"Jesse!"

He turned before opening the clinic door. Emma sprinted across the street. Ruth stood on the library steps, shading her eyes with her hand, glancing around the yard.

Jesse sighed. It didn't take a scientist to know that Tommy had taken off again.

"How long has he been gone?"

Emma stopped and gasped for breath. "Sometime during the lunch period. One of the other boys said Tommy went to check on the progress of your house."

"He should know how dangerous that is." He clenched his jaw and gripped Emma's elbow. Jesse wasn't much of one for spanking a child, but Tommy pushed his patience to the limit.

"Your grip is a bit tight," Emma tried to pull free.

"I'm sorry." He released her. "The workers dug a hole for a basement, upon my request. I'm not comfortable without one since the twister. If Tommy plays around there …"

"I understand."

The home site was two blocks from the clinic. Far enough away to provide him and Tommy with some privacy, but close enough that Jesse could get there quickly in the case of an emergency. He thanked God for giving him the foresight. "What possessed my son to leave school? Don't you watch the children during their recess?"

"The older students keep an eye on the younger students." She cut him a sideways glance. "Am I not allowed a small amount of time to take care of personal needs and eat my own lunch?"

"Not if it hinders the safety of your students." By now, they had stopped at the edge of Jesse's property, their voices raising. "We'll continue this discussion once we've found my son." He marched toward the pit marring the landscape. "Tommy!"

Emma headed for a stack of lumber a few yards away. "Tommy!"

Jesse stood on the edge of the dug out basement. The foundation and walls were standing, but no stairs. The only way in and out was a rickety ladder. At the far end was a stack of wood and boxes. A towheaded boy peeked over the top, then ducked.

Giggles filled the air. A tin can rattled across the basement floor. "Tommy Baxter, get up here this instant, and bring your friends with you."

Tommy and two other boys, faces red with perspiration, climbed the ladder and stood in front of Jesse with their heads down. Were all three of them missing after lunch? Jesse glared at Emma as she approached.

"Seth and Luke Robbins." She planted her fists on her hips. "Did you ditch school today"?"

"Yes, ma'am," they said in unison.

That answered Jesse's question. The only one Emma had been neglectful toward had been Tommy. "What are the three of you doing here?" he asked.

"Playing hide-n-go-seek," Tommy said. "It's the perfect place."

"It's a dangerous place. You should know better." He stretched out his arm and pointed. "You other boys go home. My son has some explaining to do."

Once they were gone, Jesse tilted Tommy's face up to his. "Explain."

"I just wanted to have some fun." He shrugged. "You're so busy all the time, and I don't have anyone else to play with. Seth and Luke told me what they were planning to do, so I ditched. I didn't hurt anyone."

"You could have been killed." Jesse's heart lurched. "I know I've been busy lately, so I've planned a camping trip for this weekend. How does that sound?"

"Great!" Tommy grabbed Jesse's hand, then reached for Emma's. "Miss Larson and Grandma can come too. It'll be like we're a family."

"Mercy." Emma said, under her breath.

Mercy, indeed. While Jesse was still perturbed, and

the subject of his son leaving school because of a lack of supervision wasn't a finished discussion, part one of his plan fell into place.

"I guess that's settled." He grinned.

"Don't you want to finish discussing my inadequacies?" Emma tilted her head. "Surely, you don't intend for someone as irresponsible as myself to go on something as exciting as a camping trip."

"Don't you want to go, Miss Larson?" Tommy peered up at her.

"I enjoy camping. That isn't the question here. Run on ahead of us, please."

Tommy bounded away, kicking a rock down the road.

The woman was going to drive him crazy. Jesse held out his hands in a peace offering. "I might have jumped to conclusions. I know how much your students mean to you. Finding out where Tommy had gone and knowing the danger he was in, caused me to say some hurtful things."

"You are forgiven. Now, how do you intend to discipline your son? If you're taking him camping, that can be construed as a reward."

Jesse sighed. Again, with his lack of discipline. "I'll have him clean the clinic. Will that suffice?"

She grinned, the gorgeous little imp. "Then, yes, Grandma and I will be happy to go camping with you."

He chuckled, not taking offense at her sticking her nose into his discipline abilities. Lord knew he needed all the help he could get.

18

"Grandma, please." Emma dropped the hammer in frustration. Not having ever put a tent up before, she needed help. Seeing how excited Jesse and Tommy were over going fishing, she'd volunteered to set up camp and almost instantly regretted it. Now, Grandma seemed to think it more necessary to start preparing lunch rather than put up shelter.

Emma eyed the thickening clouds overhead. They could all very well be drenched in an hour.

"Relax, dear. That's what we're here for." Grandma dug into a cardboard box. "I fried some chicken for lunch and I swear ... here it is!" She lifted a heavier box over her head. "We need to tie these things up in a tree. We don't want to encourage bears. I don't think the puppy is big enough to scare them off yet."

Bears? Emma clutched her collar and scanned the tree line. Why had she agreed to come? Because she was a sucker for a blue-eyed Baxter man, that's why.

She grabbed the hammer again and whacked at a wooden stake that was supposed to hold down a corner of the tent. The wind whipped at the canvas, fighting against Emma's attempts to settle things into place.

"I'll hold it." Grandma dropped a rock the size of

her head on the corner of the canvas. "Just move that from corner to corner." She rubbed her hands together, then planted them on her hips. "Take a big whiff of that fresh air. No automobiles up here."

Not that many in Oakton either, but Grandma wasn't the first person Emma had heard mention the noise and smells the cars produced. There! One corner down. She wiped the back of her hand across her forehead.

She had the tent up by lunchtime and collapsed into a wooden folding chair as Tommy held up a stringer of five trout. "Those will be perfect for our supper," she said.

The rain had passed, leaving an unusually warm, humid day. Fanning her face with her hand, she closed her eyes and rested her head against the chair back. She opened them long enough to eat a fried chicken leg, then closed them again and fell asleep.

When she opened them again, the sun hovered low on the horizon and Jesse squatted next to the fire. With a fork, he moved pieces of trout around in a cast iron skillet. Tommy played with a ball, throwing it so Annie could bound after it.

"Good afternoon," he said, smiling. "You must have been tired."

"Putting up that tent wore me out." She grabbed a nearby canteen and drank until the dryness left her mouth. "Where's Grandma?"

"She went into the tent a couple of hours ago. I guess she was as tired as you."

Emma stood and leaned back, popping the kinks from her neck and back before poking her head into the tent. The sleeping bags lay rolled out in military precision. A piece of canvas divided the boys' section from the girls'. Grandma wasn't on either side, but the back wall of the tent was rolled up as pretty as you pleased. Emma backed out.

"She isn't in there. She snuck out the back." Her heart lodged in her throat. "What if she gets eaten by a bear?"

"Perhaps she had business to take care of?" Jesse removed the pan from the fire and set it on a rock.

"For two hours?" Emma shook her head. "She's wandered off. I know it." She headed for a trail that led into the woods.

"Wait." Jesse shot to his feet and stopped her. "You can't go running off into the woods alone." He ducked into the tent, returning with a pistol tucked into his belt. "Tommy, tie up Annie and come with us. We can't leave you here alone."

"But you're leaving Annie." He frowned.

"She needs to protect the camp, doesn't she?"

Tommy nodded. "I didn't think of that. Good idea, Dad." He hooked a rope to Annie's collar, then tied the other end to a small sapling. Then, he slipped his hand into his father's.

"She can't have gone far," Jesse said. "I'm sure she's picking wildflowers or something."

"She's not able to go long periods of time without supervision." Hadn't they had this conversation before? Why didn't a man with a doctor's degree pay more attention?

If something happened, it was all her fault. She should never have fallen asleep. Shoving aside a low-hanging branch, she ducked past Jesse and increased her pace. She dared a bear to get in her way.

"Grandma!" She could be anywhere if she left the camp immediately. Two hours was a long time for someone to wander.

A creek rushed past a few feet ahead of them. Could Grandma swim? What if she had fallen in?

Emma dashed forward and scanned the ground for footprints. Nothing more than what looked like they belonged to Jesse or Tommy. Grandma was lost in the forest. Eaten by a bear. Wandering in a daze.

She bent over, her breath coming in quick gasps. They had to find her.

"Concentrate, Emma." Jesse put an arm around her. "One, two—"

She shrugged free. "Forget about me. Find my grandmother."

"I only want to—"

"Please." Why wouldn't he listen to her? "I'm filled with fear. It's choking me." She gripped his arms. "What if something happened to her?"

"I don't think it has." He swallowed, his Adam's apple bobbing. "There's something I need to tell you."

He couldn't be serious. He couldn't possibly be going to tell her that he knew where Grandma was. That would be a joke too cruel to contemplate. "Tell me."

~

"I don't know where she is, but I'm pretty sure she's only hiding so we have to look for her together." Jesse feared Emma would pass out, her complexion was so pale. "Together is the key word."

"I need further explanation than that." She stepped back and crossed her arms.

He never thought dark brown eyes could shoot fire,

but hers were smoldering enough that one spark could set them off. "She has this plan of getting us together before she marries Mr. Carson. I believe her wandering off is part of that plan."

"But you don't know that, do you?" Her calmness alerted him to the fact anger simmered below the surface. Add in the fact she made no mention of Ruth's plan, and he figured he might want to watch his back the rest of the day.

"Not with one hundred percent certainty, no."

"But," her eyes narrowed. "This does explain why you aren't more concerned about her welfare. Very well. Since you believe she isn't senile, but rather a master mind at matchmaking, where do you believe she is hiding?"

"The only place I can think of is a cave not too far from here." He turned and headed right, leaving Tommy to chatter nonstop to Emma. Maybe his son could brighten her mood. All Jesse seemed to do was darken it.

"Here, Miss Larson."

Jesse glanced back to see Tommy hand Emma a handful of wildflowers. The boy was a charmer for sure.

Emma smiled and sniffed them. "They're beautiful. Thank you. Maybe we should pick some more for my grandmother when we find her."

"All right." Tommy bent and grasped another bundle. "We can put these in a can when we eat supper."

Supper! Jesse's shoulders slumped. The fish wouldn't be fit to eat even if a bear didn't get to them. A bear! Annie.

"Stay here. I'll be right back." He whirled and pushed through the brush, leaving Emma and Tommy standing there with wide eyes.

He burst into the clearing where they had set up camp. The cast iron skillet was overturned. Annie's rope was snapped in two, and the puppy nowhere to be seen. Claw marks raked the side of the box containing their foodstuffs, but thankfully hadn't broken through. They'd placed the box high enough in a tree that the bear had only scratched the bottom of the box.

"Annie?"

A black snout on a golden nose peeked from under the tent. Annie whimpered.

"You poor thing. That bear scared you enough to give you the strength to break free, didn't it?" He found another rope suitable for a leash, tied it around the dog's neck, and raced back to Emma and Tommy. If something had happened to the dog, Emma would never have forgiven him.

"What happened?" Emma held out her hand for the leash, then bent to hug the dog instead. "Why, she's trembling."

"A bear ate our supper, knocked over our stools, and scared the puppy. It could have been a lot worse. Let's go find Ruth."

He led them another ten minutes down the path, then veered to the right and up a small incline. At the top, nestled behind some huckleberry bushes, was the entrance to a small cave.

Removing his pistol, he held out a hand to stop them. "Let me go first. Bears like these berries and sometimes claim the cave as their home."

"Grandma." Emma put a hand over her mouth.

Jesse put a hand to his lips, then carefully moved toward the cave's entrance. "Ruth?"

"Hello!" She popped up from behind the bushes. "You found me."

He shook his head, motioning for her to settle down. If she acted too chipper, Emma was bound to discredit his explanation of a plan to get them together and stick to her idea of Ruth being senile. "Your granddaughter is not happy with you."

"Oh, pooh. She'll thank me someday." She grinned and headed down the hill to Emma. "Wonderful day for a hike."

Emma peered over her shoulder at Jesse as if to say, "See? Senile."

"What were you thinking? You could have been injured or killed. Then, what would I have done?" She slipped her arm through Ruth's. "You can't scare me like that. I might have wanted to hike with you."

"You hiked with Jesse. That's much better." She patted Emma's hand. "I'm starving."

"A bear ate our fish," Tommy said.

"Gracious! How exciting." Ruth hugged him with her free arm. "We should try catching some more."

"It's getting dark."

"Fish love the dark." She pulled free from Emma and moved ahead with Tommy.

"She worries me."

"There is nothing wrong with her mind, Emma." Jesse replaced his pistol in his waistband. "She's as sharp as you or I."

"No, she asked me to come and take care of her because she couldn't take care of herself." She peered up at him. "Why would she say that if it weren't true?"

"You dear woman. Can't you see? She doesn't want you to be alone. This whole wandering off and acting childish is nothing but a ploy to get you and I together. If you ask her, the twister was the best thing that happened to us."

"If she thinks that way, then she really is losing her mind." Emma exhaled sharply and resumed walking.

Which part of what he said did she refer to? The part of them getting together or the part about the twister? She didn't seem excited at the concept of him and her getting together or the fact that Ruth might pretend an illness in order to get them together. If she were to ever find out that Jesse was a willing participant in the deception, all hopes of her accepting his attentions would be gone.

When they reached camp, Ruth and Tommy gathered up the fishing equipment and a lantern before heading for the creek and more fish.

Emma watched them go, then turned to Jesse. "All right. You may be correct in your assumptions. So, what are we going to do to let my grandmother know that her silly plan won't do any good?"

Jesse's heart dropped.

19

Emma crawled from the tent the next morning. Instead of answering her question the night before regarding Grandma's ridiculous plan, Jesse had frowned and stormed away. Surely, he didn't think they should get married without a word of love spoken and just because an old woman wished it?

No, Emma wanted declarations of love. She wanted a man she could trust with her heart. She thought Jesse could be that man, especially with the way her traitorous heart stuttered every time he walked into view or smiled her way. But, he'd never come out and said that he desired Emma for anything more than a friend and a teacher to his son.

"Coffee?" Jesse held out a blue tin mug with white specks.

"Thank you." She accepted the cup and sat in a folding chair. "You never answered my question last night."

"I don't have an answer, Emma." A shadow passed over his face. "Is it such a bad thing to humor her?"

"If she's living a fantasy, yes."

He shook his head. "Why are you so convinced she's touched in the head?"

She didn't know for sure, but one of Grandma's neighbors had informed Emma upon her arrival that Ruth Larson was crazier than a rabid bat. Of course, that neighbor had left Oakton shortly after the twister, so Emma couldn't dig further into the details. Not to mention Grandma's childlike approach to life. Could it be possible that Emma was older in her actions than her grandmother? The thought saddened her.

"More fish." Grandma breezed down the path, a stringer full of trout in her hand. "We've supper again tonight and enough for breakfast in the morning before heading home." She glanced from Emma to Jesse. "Why the long faces? It's a glorious day."

"I'm not fully awake," Emma said, lifting her mug. She needed to have a serious conversation with Grandma, sooner rather than later, but it would have to wait until they returned to town. She wouldn't ruin their vacation by broaching a subject that might result in hurt feelings.

"Take a walk with me after breakfast," Grandma said. The look on her face was sterner than any Emma had seen on her before.

The only sound at breakfast was Tommy's chatter to Annie and the birds singing in the trees. Emma glanced several times at Grandma, but she avoided her gaze every time. Emma felt like a child awaiting punishment. Maybe she was. Maybe her own insecurities had confused her and filled her with unnecessary fears. *God, have I been wrong about everything?*

She took her plate of scrambled eggs and her coffee mug into the tent. She needed time alone with her thoughts. What kind of person believed the accusations of a stranger without first consulting their loved one? Grandma's zest for life could be simply that. Her childish ways didn't have to mean she was going senile.

She set her dishes down and covered her face with her hands. What a fool. Why did she act the way she did? Did she not think herself good enough to be loved unless she was first needed? Bill hadn't loved her, not really.

She glanced out the open tent flap at Jesse. He didn't seem averse to people thinking the two of them were an item, but love wasn't an issue with him either. Was Emma not worthy of love other than the unconditional love of God? Where did she go from here?

Soon, she'd have no job. Grandma would be married. Emma would be alone. No holds or responsibilities outside of her job. An unanchored ship tossed in life's ocean. Was she destined to be a spinster?

She wanted love, marriage, children. She gazed on Jesse's strong, handsome form hunkered by the fire. She wanted him. But, only if he wanted, loved, desired her in return.

"I'm ready, child." Grandma poked her head into the tent. "Let's take a walk."

Emma sighed, carried her half eaten breakfast to the bucket they'd brought along for dirty dishes, grabbed the bucket, then followed her grandmother down the path toward the creek. She might as well clean up while they talked.

"Set the bucket down and look at me."

Emma did as instructed. Now, she really did feel

like a child.

"I don't know what you've got fixed in your mind, girlie, but you need to get your thoughts straightened out." Grandma motioned for her to sit on a fallen log. "I'm marrying Mr. Carson early this summer. That will leave you alone to pursue whatever it is you want to pursue, whether it be a career or a family."

"Your neighbors said you were crazy." Emma sat.

Grandma laughed. "They caught me dancing among the laundry hanging on the line one day. It was the first time Mr. Carson asked me out to dinner. I suppose I looked a bit crazy."

"So, you really don't need me." Emma's heart fell to her knees.

Grandma sat next to her and pulled her into a hug. "No, I don't, but I do love you with every fiber of my being. Can't you relax and enjoy life? Stop thinking so hard, sweetie. It isn't good for you."

She rested her head on Grandma's shoulder and watched the sun's rays dapple the water with light. It really was a pretty place. "I'm trying not to be so…rigid, but I've had to be a grown-up my entire life. I don't know how to let loose."

"I'm sorry about that. Your father was an old man the day he was born. I don't know where that personality trait came from. Just promise me, you won't die bitter and alone someday."

She straightened. "Are you purposely trying to get me and Jesse together?"

"Of course." She grinned. "You'd never think of it on your own."

~

Jesse glanced at the path more times than he

wanted to admit, waiting for a sign that the women were returning. Was Ruth admitting to her plan of getting him and Emma together? What would be Emma's reaction?

"Is Miss Larson mad at us?" Tommy tossed the ball into the tent for Annie to fetch.

"I don't think so. Why?" Jesse kicked dirt over the coals of their fire.

"She didn't say anything at breakfast."

"Maybe she isn't a morning person."

Tommy shrugged. "I guess. I was hoping she would be my new mommy. I like her. Do you?"

"Yes, I like her very much." But, he didn't like the way the conversation was going. He needed to change the subject before Tommy took it upon himself to let Emma know of his father's feelings for her. Until she seemed more receptive to the idea of them being together, he couldn't voice how his heart beat faster when he saw her or the way her brown eyes reminded him of chocolate and everything good.

Laughter rang out seconds before the women stepped into view. So, the conversation had been a good one.

"Dishes are done." Emma grinned and moved past him to set the bucket next to the tent. "What are our plans for today?"

"There's a waterfall I want to show you." His heart stopped, waiting for her answer.

"I think we would all enjoy that." She tilted her head, her dark gaze searching his face. When he didn't say anything further, she went to tie the box high into the tree.

So, it was to be all four of them. Fine. He'd take

her company however he could get it. "It's settled then. Tommy, put the leash on Annie. She's coming with us."

Somehow, someway, he needed to get his feelings across to Emma without actually telling her. He couldn't face her rejection or her pity if she didn't feel the same way. If he showed her without saying anything, then he could salvage a bit of pride if she didn't return his sentiments.

"You're as easy to read as a book with large print," Ruth said, tying the tent flap closed. "Just say something to her." She groaned. "You two must be the most stubborn people in the Ozarks. You should have outright told her the waterfall was a hike for two. Romance is wasted on the young." She stormed away.

She was right, and it was too late to change things now. Jesse retrieved his pistol, scanned the campsite for anything that might attract unwanted visitors, then called out for the other three to join him.

"There are areas where a bit of climbing might be necessary. Let me go first to make sure the path is stable." He grabbed the canteen, and a pack with their lunches, then led the way away from camp.

He'd find a way to sit and speak nonsense to Emma at the waterfall. Maureen hadn't been the romantic kind. What did a man say to a woman who wanted sweet nothings whispered to her? It was as foreign to him as the thought of wearing ribbons in his hair.

His foot slipped on some loose leaves. "Watch your footing." He turned and held out his hand to help Emma down the muddy decline.

"Oh." Her feet slid. Her arms windmilled.

He grabbed her and spun, stopping their fall

against the rock face of a cliff. Her lips were close enough to kiss. Her lips parted and her breath tickled his face. Would she slap him? He lowered his head.

"Dad! Come help Grandma."

His son's words ripped him from the moment. He released his hold on Emma and turned to help Ruth. It was for the best. He didn't want their first kiss to be with an audience cheering them on.

"Like I said," Ruth commented as he helped her down. "Romance is wasted on the young. That is a moment you might not get back." She shook her head and stepped to the side so he could continue to lead the way.

He heard the waterfall before he saw it. With rain higher up on the mountain the last few days, the water cascaded down into a crystal pool. "Take off your shoes," he shouted above the noise. "It'll be cold, but refreshing."

He sat next to Emma and toed off his shoes and peeled off his socks. "No repeat of our last water adventure, please." He grinned.

"Then, you, sir, should mind your distance." She smiled and got to her feet, the legs of her pants rolled to her knees.

She made a delightful picture in baggy pants and a man's shirt two sizes too big for her. He wanted to ask where she'd found the clothes, but thought it too personal.

Frigid water splashed his face, stopping him from staring. "Hey!"

Emma laughed and tried to run. Keep his distance indeed. He bounded after her, the coldness of the water taking his breath away. Or was it the giggling woman in front of him that made it hard for him to catch his breath? He didn't care who was watching. When he caught her, he fully intended to kiss her.

He slipped on moss under his feet and went down, fully submerging himself. He came up sputtering to see Emma doubled over in laughter. One swipe of his foot, and she was down, too.

The current carried them into the pool. He grabbed her to him before she could resurface and pressed his lips against hers. Locked together, they floated to the top, her arms snaking around his neck.

He smiled into the kiss. It was everything he'd thought it would be.

The moment they surfaced, she slipped her arms free and swam away, leaving him colder than the water's temperature. What was she so afraid of?

20

Emma put her chilled hands to her hot face. She hadn't noticed the coldness of the water; not during the kiss, but the moment she pulled away, shivers took over.

Jesse grabbed her arm and pulled her behind the jutting roots of a tree. "Marry me."

"What?" Surely, she hadn't heard him correctly.

"Marry me."

"Why?" *Say you love me.* That's all it would take for her to throw herself into his arms.

He hesitated. "Don't deny that the kiss moved you."

"Of course it did. I'm a young woman being kissed by a handsome man." He wasn't going to say the words she longed to hear. She kept her gaze glued on his face. When the words didn't come, she turned away to hide her tears.

"I know you care for Tommy. He needs a mother, Emma. You already fit in our family so well."

She shook her head and moved away, measuring her grief by the deepness of the water. As the water receded, her sadness grew. No mention of love, other than what she felt for his adorable child. That wasn't enough to base a lifetime together on. Not nearly enough. All it would take was three little words.

"What's wrong?" Grandma reached for her hand and helped her to the bank.

"I'm not feeling well. I'd like to return to camp." Emma sat on a large rock and put on her socks and shoes.

"We're heading back," Grandma called to Jesse. "I'll leave the food basket for you and Tommy."

Jesse nodded, staying in the water until Emma stood. She glanced at him, then headed down the path. If Grandma listened hard enough, she'd be able to hear Emma's heart breaking over the whisper of the wind in the trees.

The only solution to her pain was to make arrangements to move to Harrisburg as soon as school let out for the summer. The recital was next week, on the last day of school. That gave her seven, maybe eight days to move on from the pain of Oakton.

Grandma, bless her heart, remained silent on the thirty minute hike back to camp. But that's where giving Emma her privacy ended. She followed Emma into the tent. "Tell me what's really going on. You aren't prone to headaches."

She sagged onto one of the sleeping bags. "Jesse asked me to marry him."

"That's wonderful!" Grandma clapped her hands.

"No." Emma raised her head. "He only wants a mother for his son. Not once did he say he loved me, or even cares for me. Only that I was a perfect fit for his family."

Grandma sat next to her. "Some men aren't good with flowery words."

"All I want is to hear him say he loves me. I won't marry anyone without those words."

"Have you told him how you feel?"

"I can't. After Bill's deception, I can't be the first to express my feelings. That turned out to be a disaster."

"Not all men are like Bill." She put an arm around Emma's shoulders. "Your grandfather was a wonderful man. Mr. Carson is also a true treasure. Be honest, honey. With yourself and with Jesse."

She leaned her head against Grandma's. "I'm so afraid of being hurt."

"That fear is keeping you from living the way you're intended to. Give your worries to God and see what wonders you experience."

If only it were that simple. Her father, while he had loved her in his distant way, hadn't been one to show affection. Then, when Bill cheated on her, Emma had built a wall around her heart. Jesse had chipped away at the bricks, piece-by-piece. Now, he wanted a marriage of convenience, and she wasn't sure she was capable of protecting herself during such a partnership.

She stood. "I'm ready to go home." Ignoring her grandmother's pleas, Emma started rolling up the sleeping bags and tying them together. By the time Jesse and Tommy had returned, the tent was torn down and secured on top of the car.

Jesse's eyes widened when he returned, but to his credit, he said nothing, only explaining to Tommy that Emma didn't feel well and they were returning to town a little early. She smiled sadly as a thank you and dumped water on the fire to make sure it was definitely out before they left.

"I apologize for whatever I said that upset you so," he whispered over her shoulder.

She turned and stared at him, clutching the handle of the bucket so tight, her fingers ached. "The fact that you have no idea what you said, or how it affects me, hurts more than the words you didn't say."

He scratched his chin. "I'm confused."

She growled and shoved past him, blinking back traitorous tears that seemed to be her constant companion of late. She tossed the bucket into the floorboard of the car and slid into the backseat. Grandma could sit up front. Emma needed distance from the object of her despair.

Tommy didn't seem to mind. In fact, he was thrilled to share the back with Emma and Annie. The puppy sat between them, tongue lolling. Once the car started moving, she ran from one side to the other to hang her head out the window.

Elbow propped on the door frame, chin in hand, Emma watched the landscape roll past and contemplated her lonely future. Thank goodness, she had a job.

Jesse parked in front of their temporary home, then exited the car to unlock the door. "There are several letters on the floor. Be careful walking inside."

Emma stooped on her way in and gathered the mail, tossing all but one onto the table. She ripped into the letter from the Missouri school board and scanned the typed words. No. She was out of a job due to lack of students.

Crumbling the letter in her hand, she dashed outside and into the woods.

~

Jesse moved to dash after her, stopping when Ruth put a hand on his arm.

"Let her be," she said, thrusting a sleeping bag into his arms. "She has some things to work out for herself. Decisions only she can make."

He nodded, like he understood. In actuality, he was as confused as a child who received a scolding not knowing what they'd done wrong.

It couldn't be the kiss they'd shared by the waterfall. She had returned it with as much passion as he thought she possessed under her schoolmarm demeanor. But, just as quickly as things had grown hot, she turned cold and stormed away, declaring she didn't feel well.

Maybe he was also in need of some time alone with his thoughts. There had to be sense made out of the day somewhere, somehow. With one more glance in the direction Emma disappeared, he unloaded the car and stored the camping gear in his section of the railroad car.

"Hey, Doc!"

"Mr. Carson." Jesse smiled. "You here to see Ruth?"

"Yep, and to let you know your house is almost finished. The guys are holding off on Miss Larson's until they find out whether she's staying or moving. They sent me to find out."

"She isn't here right now. I'll have Ruth find out and let you know. Let me fetch your lady for you." Jesse entered their home. "You've got company."

Ruth wiped her hands on a dishtowel, then smoothed her hair into place. "We're making our final wedding preparations. Isn't it exciting? Imagine, a woman of my age as giddy as a schoolgirl over getting married." Her smile faded. "If you'd do right by my granddaughter, we could make it a double wedding."

"I haven't the foggiest idea what I've done wrong."

"And, I'm not the one to tell you." She patted his cheek, a bit rough. "Figure it out before it's too late."

Why couldn't someone just tell him? "Ruth, please."

"Son, if the two of you can't learn to communicate without the help of this old woman, then you aren't meant to be together. Spend some time in thought and prayer. It'll come to you." She cupped his face. "Be brutally honest with yourself. Search your heart."

He nodded and watched her join her future husband. Be honest with himself. Wasn't he usually? Regardless of Ruth's advise to let Emma be, he needed to speak with her. He told Tommy to stay put, mentioned to Ruth he was stepping out, then headed down the street.

"Good afternoon, Dr. Baxter." Fred Harper stopped him. "I'm hoping you're open for business today. I got a splinter in my foot the other evening and it's starting to fester."

Jesse glanced at the tree line, then back at Fred. "Can you hobble to my office?"

"Yep. Made myself a crutch." He grabbed a Y-shaped stick and headed for the clinic.

By the time Jesse cleaned and bandaged the foot, the sun was setting in the sky and the smells of supper cooking drifted from home. He sent Fred on his way, straightened up his supplies, and went home.

Emma stirred something at the stove. "You may

read the letter I received," she said, without turning around. "I apologize for running away. I was distraught."

He took a seat and read the letter, his heart sinking to discover she didn't have a job after all. "Have you given more thought to my proposition?"

"I'm thinking on it." She dished up a ladle of soup and handed him a bowl without meeting his gaze. "Tommy has already eaten and is playing with Annie in the other room."

She filled another bowl and sat across from him. Several times she glanced up as if she were going to say something, then looked back at her soup.

Each time, his heart leaped in anticipation. Would she say yes? He hoped so, although the thought of marrying again scared him to death. What if he couldn't keep her safe? What if he lost her as he had Maureen? Maybe proposing marriage hadn't been a good idea after all.

They needed something else to think about. "How do you feel about Ruth's impending marriage?"

"As long as Grandma is happy, I'm happy." She dipped a slice of bread into her bowl. "Mr. Carson seems like a fine man."

"One of the best. I wouldn't have any qualms about a family member of mine marrying him."

She set her spoon on the table, lining it up with her bowl. She took a deep breath, then lifted her gaze. "I, uh, excuse me." She pushed away from the table and went behind the privacy curtain.

Jesse stood and cleared the table. Whatever Emma was trying to say wasn't easy for her.

He glanced again at the letter on the table. If she

didn't marry him, what was she going to do? Move farther from Ruth in search of a teaching position? Perhaps she could stay in Oakton and find employment here. The library? She'd never answered him in regards to working in his clinic. Could he work with her if she refused his marriage proposal?

Definitely not. He set the dishes on the washboard and headed to his room.

"Time for bed, Tommy. Go wash up and put on your pajamas."

"Okay, Dad." He jumped up from where he played marbles on the floor.

"Don't forget the marbles. We don't want to trip over them in the night."

"Right." He scooped up the multi-colored circles of glass, dropped them into a drawstring bag, and set them in a crate at the foot of his bed.

Jesse kicked off his shoes and watched his son prepare for bed. They were doing all right, just the two of them. But, Tommy was young. Little more than a baby in the eyes of some people. He needed a mother. Did Jesse need a wife that didn't love him? If it would help his son, then, yes.

He fell asleep praying that Emma would be that wife and mother. If only he could figure out what it was he hadn't done.

21

"May I have your attention, please?" Emma clapped her hands to direct her students' focus on her. "This is our last week of the school year and our recital is on Friday. We will be doing our final exams and practicing for our big event. It is imperative that you attend school each day this week. Are there any questions?"

No one raised their hand. Smiles turned to frowns as their demeanors matched the way Emma felt. A few more days together and the familiar would be traded for something new, and she was no closer to figuring out her future than she had been on the camping trip.

As the children worked on an arithmetic exam, she drew a line down a sheet of paper and titled each column Pros and Cons of staying in Oakton. On the pro side, she'd be closer to Grandma. On the con side, her grandmother no longer needed her, if she ever had. Pro? She tapped her fingernail on her desk. She would be close to Jesse. Con? She would be close to Jesse.

She had nowhere else to go. If she stayed, each day would be a torment as one, she either married Jesse out of necessity or two, watched him choose someone else. If she left, she started all over in her quest for a job and a career. Perhaps Little Rock would have a teaching position. But, she didn't want to drive an hour each way when she visited Grandma. She didn't have a car and cab fare would eat up her salary.

Burying her head in her hands, she let the scratch of the students' pencils ease the frustration inside her. She had a week before making a decision, several months if she chose to wait through the summer, and didn't mind living in a tin box during the hottest part of the year.

She sighed and stood, erasing the morning's spelling from the board. One-by-one, her students brought her their exam papers, grabbed their lunch pails, and headed outside.

Emma followed, standing on the library steps. If she left, she would miss Oakton more than she'd ever thought possible. The small mountain town with its one Main Street and friendly citizens had burrowed into her heart and set up home.

As she gazed upon the street, noting the rebuilding and how quickly things were returning to normal after the twister's devastation, Jesse stepped out of his temporary clinic and headed across the street to his new one. All the new building lacked was a coat of paint and his shingle announcing the clinic.

The new mercantile had received a fresh coat of barn-red paint. Rocking chairs graced the front of the store and, sometime while they'd been camping, someone had installed a single gasoline pump.

Emma smiled. The town was becoming modern. It wouldn't surprise her if someday soon, streetlights lit up Main Street at dusk.

Jesse glanced her way as he crossed the street once

again, emerging this time with a box. Two men, also loaded with boxes, followed him. He stocked the new clinic. Soon, the railroad company would come to retrieve the donated railroad cars and Emma would once again be without a roof over her head. Worse case scenario, she moved in with Grandma and Mr. Carson.

She shuddered. That would put her in close proximity to Bill each time he came to visit.

Who was she kidding? She had made her decision while listing the pros and cons of staying. She would give Jesse her answer that evening. She rang the bell, signaling the end of lunch and recess and ushered the students inside for recital practice.

By the end of the day, her nerves were strung tight. What if Jesse got angry? Changed his mind? Kicked her and Grandma out of their temporary abode? Her head ached with all the questions.

Tommy dashed ahead and into the clinic, returning seconds later with a frown on his face. "Dad said we're moving into the old clinic until our house is finished to give you women privacy." He kicked a rock, sending it into the grass beside the road.

"Don't you want your father all to yourself again?"

He shook his head. "No. I want you to live with us forever and be my new mommy."

With those words, Emma sighed, her heart breaking. "Let's wait and see what happens, all right?"

"Sure." He scuffed his feet in the dirt all the way home.

Emma's heart beat faster the closer they got. She prayed she was doing the right thing.

Prayer. She needed to spend a few minutes with God before facing Jesse. "Go on inside, Tommy, and see whether Grandma baked any cookies. I'll be in in a bit."

The moment he left her sight, she followed the well-worn path to the lake and perched on the bench. *God, show me what to do.*

As she waited, a white crane settled on a small rock jutting above the surface of the water, peace descended over her. She *had* made the right decision, she knew that now. Whether Jesse loved her or not would not change her mind. God had settled in her mind the path she was to take with her future.

She stood, took a deep breath, and watched as the crane took flight, carrying her worries with it. She smiled and turned back toward town.

She found Jesse in his new clinic, placing medicine in a shiny glass cabinet. "Do you have a moment?" she asked.

"Of course." He waved her toward a chair. "Have a seat, please."

"I'd rather stand." She wrinkled the hem of her blouse with her hands, pulling it free from the waist of her skirt. "I have an answer for you."

His eyes brightened. "Perhaps I should be the one to sit." He plopped into a chair.

She squared her shoulders, took another deep breath, and began. "Please do not interrupt me until I've had my say."

He nodded.

"I have thought and prayed about your proposal, and while no words of love have been said, I have decided to accept your offer." Her knuckles hurt, so tight did she grasp her blouse. "I will marry you. I know your offer was out of compassion for my homeless, jobless situation, and that you need a mother for Tommy, so I have decided to accept."

Why wasn't he saying anything?

~

It wasn't exactly the acceptance he had dreamed of, but he would take Emma Larson anyway he could get her. He stood and walked around the desk, taking her hands in his.

"My, dear, sweet, beautiful Emma. I'm not one to know what to say if I'm not speaking in medical terms." He knelt in front of her, his gaze locked on hers. "I'm sorry I never said I loved you. Can't you see it in my eyes? Ruth was right. That twister was the best thing that ever happened to me. It brought me you. Let me ask you again, with declarations of love … Emma Larson, will you marry me?"

Tears filled her eyes. "You aren't asking out of pity? Or convenience?"

"No," he chuckled. "I'm asking out of love. If all I want is a mother for my son, I could hire a nanny. Well? Please answer before my knees sport permanent bruises."

Her shoulders shook, whether with sobs or laughter, he wasn't sure. "Yes," she said. "I'll marry you for love."

He stood and pulled her into his arms. "I can't promise to shower you with words of romance or that I'll be home every night. I'm a doctor. My job will pull me away and fill my mind with anything but romance." He tilted her chin until she faced him. "But, I will promise to love you."

"That's all I ask."

"I didn't keep Maureen safe." His breath hitched.

"I'll do my best, but —"

She placed her finger on his lips. "That isn't something you can always control. I trust you with my heart and my life, Jesse Baxter."

"Let's go tell our families." He ran his hands down her arms, relishing in the silkiness of her skin. Soon, every inch of her would be his. "But first, I want to kiss you."

"I was beginning to wonder if we were going to seal our engagement with a kiss or not." Her eyes sparkled with humor.

He lowered his head and pulled her closer as his lips landed on hers. Her arms wound around his neck as she plastered herself so close to him that their shadows melded into one.

A soft moan escaped her throat, doing things to him that he hadn't felt since Maureen. He gave God a silent prayer of thanksgiving and deepened the kiss. It wasn't until her knees weakened that he lifted his head.

"How was that for sealing the deal?"

Her lips spread into a seductive smile. "If you kiss me like that every morning and every evening, I'll never have reason to doubt your love."

Cheers and clapping pulled their attention to the window. A crowd had gathered.

Jesse laughed. A new plate glass window didn't afford a man a lot of privacy in which to kiss his girl. He waved, then dipped Emma over his arm to more cheers. "Let's go meet our fans."

Her face turned a delightful shade of pink. "I'm mortified."

"Darling, we've just gotten started giving this town something to talk about." He set her back on her feet and took her hand. "Ready?"

She nodded.

The crowd cheered louder when they stepped outside. "I reckon there's going to be a wedding," someone yelled.

"There is!" Jesse held his and Emma's hand up. "A double wedding, if Ruth and Jim don't mind."

"Not a bit." Jim Carson put an arm around Ruth's shoulders. "We've been wondering whether you would ever get around to asking her."

Emma pressed against his side. "It was me dragging my feet," she said. "So, when's the wedding?"

"Saturday!"

She trembled and glanced up at Jesse. "This Saturday?"

He grinned. "Yep. The day after the recital. You might want to find a dress."

He was the luckiest man in the Ozarks, marrying the prettiest woman. He glanced to his right and spotted Tommy with tears running down his face. "Come here, son." He held out his arms.

"I'm getting a new mommy." Tommy launched himself at Jesse. "I asked her just today."

"You did?" Jesse looked over his head at Emma.

"He did. That made my decision."

"You were going to give up your dreams for my son?" Was it possible to love her more?

"I didn't give up anything." She caressed his face. "My dream is standing in front of me."

The crowd dispersed the moment Jesse led his family into their home. Temporary home. He had it on good authority that his house would be complete by the weekend. He was sure the workers could have it ready for him to carry Emma inside after the wedding.

"What are you thinking about?" Emma hung her school bag on a hook.

"On whether the pastor's wife will let Tommy spend the night with them on Saturday." He laughed as Emma's face darkened.

"Grandma said she was … a bit mixed up?"

"Tommy will only need her to tuck him in. The pastor will be there." He drew her into an embrace. "Mrs. Richardson is fine. Just a little shell-shocked from the storm and getting better every day." He tapped her nose. "I don't want our wedding night to be spent with a six-year-old."

"I'm almost seven," Tommy piped in from the back room. "I don't mind staying with Pastor as long as Annie can come."

Jesse leaned his forehead against Emma's. "Saturday won't come fast enough."

"For you maybe. I have a lot to do to get ready." She smiled and pulled back. "I think tonight warrants a meal at the diner."

"I agree." He called for Tommy, took Emma's hand, and feeling as if the three of them were already a family, stepped into the warm spring evening.

Thank you. He glanced heavenward.

22

"Hush, children. The curtain goes up in five minutes. Take your places." Emma pulled Tommy away from the opening. She didn't blame them for their excitement. They'd all worked hard on the spring recital.

She smiled. Not only that, but tomorrow was her wedding day. She would be a wife and a mother, helping Jesse in his clinic until Oakton once again had a school. She'd found her place to belong. How could she ever have thought of leaving?

She bent and picked up Tommy's paper. He'd written a small tribute to his mother, one that would bring the audience to tears, if she weren't mistaken. She'd shed a few of her own upon reading it.

Murmurs increased on the other side of the quilts hung as curtains, signaling the audience was getting restless. Everyone who had a student in school, and many others out for a night of simple entertainment, had bought tickets. After much debate, Emma had chosen to sell the tickets to help purchase books for the library. It was the least she could do after holding school there for the last few months.

The curtains parted. Emma glanced one more time

at the excited children, then stepped back. This was their moment to shine.

The program opened with a group singing of *America, the Beautiful*. Then, one-by-one, the students stepped forward and performed something they considered their greatest achievement of the year.

They had everything from songs and poems, to the reciting of the multiplication tables up to twelve. When Tommy stepped forward, he held up his hands for the applause to quiet, then read of how much he loved his mother. Sniffles and hankies were in high abundance.

"But," he said, holding his paper down, "God has given me a new mommy. One that makes my Dad smile again. Tomorrow, Miss Emma Larson will be my mommy." He held out his hand and wiggled his fingers.

With tears streaming down her face, Emma stepped forward and took his hand in hers. "That was beautiful."

She faced the audience. "That ends our spring recital. I hope you are proud of your children's accomplishments. They've worked hard this year, despite attending school for extra time due to time missed because of the twister." Would she always think of that time as the 'Time of the Twister'?

Her gaze fell on the beaming face of her betrothed. She returned his smile, then focused once again on the audience. "Refreshments are served on tables set up outside. I have been blessed to have taught your children this year. Thank you." She bowed and backed up as the curtains closed to thunderous applause.

"Students." Emma clapped her hands. "May God bless you this summer and into the next school year. Remember ... if you have any problems with your next year's assignments, come find me. I would love to tutor you. You are dismissed."

Each student thrust a rose in her hand as they passed, causing her tears to start fresh. Oh, how she would miss them. Still, she was entering a new chapter in her own life and wouldn't have time for much more than tutoring. At least not in the beginning.

"Sweetheart, that was fabulous." Grandma, escorted by Jim and Jesse, stepped onto the makeshift stage. "You did a fine job with these children."

"Thank you." Emma gave her a quick hug, then slipped her arm through Jesse's. "I think Tommy is excited about tomorrow."

"No more so than I." He planted a quick kiss on her lips. "Let's get some refreshments before they're all gone."

The moment they stepped outside, those who had watched the recital applauded again with cheers. While Emma would see them all again tomorrow at her and Grandma's wedding, it thrilled her to know how much the community had come to love her.

Her, Emma Larson, the serious schoolteacher who hadn't known fun until arriving in Oakton. While she'd thought she had come to help, she had been the one needing rescuing.

Her handsome knight released her hold and dashed away to fetch her refreshments while she greeted her royal subjects. Not that Emma was a princess, but at that moment, she felt like one. She didn't think she would ever quit smiling.

~

Head swimming, heart pounding, Emma plopped onto the bench in the back room of the newly built church. She leaned forward, putting her head between her knees. Not even the twister had frightened her so. No, frightened wasn't the right word. She was overly excited. Shaky from not eating breakfast. Her nerves twanged.

"Eat this." Grandma thrust a slice of raisin bread into her hands. "We've got to get you on your feet and dressed."

Emma peered up. "You look beautiful."

Grandma stood in front of her with a new blue suit and snappy hat with a short veil covering half of her face.

"Thank you. But, you, my dear, will outshine me. If, we can get you dressed." Grandma lifted the white silk gown from a hook. "Tetched in the head or not, Delores can sew up a storm."

The gown was the prettiest thing Emma had ever seen. It fell in a shimmering wave to her hips, then cascaded out to swish around her ankles. The veil was as long as the dress and adorned with white roses. Nervousness forgotten, Emma reached out to take the dress.

"Not until you eat and wash your hands." Grandma held it an arm's length away.

Emma chuckled. Nothing swept away nerves like Grandma's no-nonsense attidute. And to think Emma had thought her going senile.

She quickly ate the bread, then washed her hands in the bowl provided. Fortified, she dropped her robe and turned to Grandma. "I'm ready."

The dress slid over her skin like butter. It was a miracle Mrs. Richardson had finished it in time. The dress and the slip underneath should have taken much longer than a month to make.

"Beautiful." Grandma stepped back and clasped her hands. "A true vision. Jesse will be dumbstruck."

Emma turned and looked in the mirror. Her dark hair and eyes provided a pleasing contrast to the soft white of the dress. "I'm ready," she whispered. "Thank you, God."

Grandma handed her a simple bouquet of white roses. "Let's get married."

The strains of the wedding march started in the sanctuary. Emma leaned over and planted a kiss on Grandma's cheek. "I don't know what I would have done if you hadn't written for me to come."

"Pine away in lonely foolishness." She smiled.

Together, they strolled through the double doors and down the aisle.

Emma's gaze locked with Jesse's. His eyes drew her like a beacon. She'd been lost in the storm and he was her light. She stepped next to him and placed her hand in his as Pastor Richardson began to speak.

"Dearly Beloved …"

The End

DEAR READER

In 1925, a tornado that would be known as the Tri-State Tornado, touched down in Ellington, Missouri and continued its path of destruction into Indiana, leaving behind hundreds of deaths and many homes destroyed. On today's Fujita scale, this twister would be an F5. There was no warning, other than an exceptionally warm day in March.

While the characters and town in *The Teacher's Rescue* are fictitious, I hope I have shown the strength and fortitude of the people affected by this twister. For the sake of the story, I embellished a bit by adding a second tornado. Railroad cars really were donated as temporary housing, and people, and homes, were picked up and set back down, some with only minor injuries or damage.

I hope you enjoyed reading this story as much as I enjoyed writing it.

Cynthia Hickey

ABOUT THE AUTHOR

www.cynthiahickey.com

Cynthia Hickey is a multi-published and best-selling author of cozy mysteries and romantic suspense. She has taught writing at many conferences and small writing retreats. She and her husband run the publishing press, Winged Publications. They live in Arizona and Arkansas, becoming snowbirds with three dogs. They have ten grandchildren who keep them busy and tell everyone they know that "Nana is a writer."

www.ingramcontent.com/pod-product-compliance
Lightning Source LLC
LaVergne TN
LVHW010325070526
838199LV00065B/5657